CHAPTER ONE

GEORGIE MCARTHUR pulled herself up the almost vertical rock face, inch by painful inch. The day that had started with unseasonably warm sun was now, in true Scottish spring fashion, beginning to close in and the temperature was dropping rapidly. Despite the chill in the air, Georgie could feel perspiration beading her brow as she willed her stiff and unused muscles higher up the cliff. Taking a deep breath, she dug her fingertips into the rock and, finding the narrowest of footholds, dragged herself another couple of inches closer.

The ledge she was heading for was now only two feet above her and slightly to the right. This last bit of the climb was critical and she prayed the injured boy would stay still until she reached him. If he panicked now and the shelf crumbled, it could send him tumbling over the edge—and her along with him.

'Stay as still as you can,' she called out. 'I'll be with you soon, but I have to climb above you first. Okay?' There was no reply. The child was hidden from her view by the ledge and Georgie fervently hoped he was all right.

Steadying herself, she continued climbing until she was above him. At last she could see him clearly. He was sitting huddled against the cliff wall, his legs in front of him, the left twisted at an unnatural angle. Without doubt it was broken, but how badly? The boy was pale and clearly distressed.

'Almost there—just sit tight,' Georgie said, inserting another bolt into the cliff. By climbing higher than the boy, she could suspend herself just above him until she made an assessment of the stability of the shelf of rock. The last thing she wanted was for her added weight to send them both plummeting to the ground.

Finally she was in position. The boy had been watching her wide-eyed while she'd made her preparations. He looked about nine years old, and his anxious, pain-filled eyes tugged at her heart. He was so little to be going through this on his own. Which begged the question: where was the adult—or adults—who had been with him? As far as Georgie knew, the call had come from a climber who had just happened to be passing when he'd spotted the brightly coloured jacket the boy was wearing. He'd immediately called the rescue services.

It had been Georgie's bad luck to be visiting her brother Kirk at the mountain rescue clubhouse when the call had come through. The timing was all off. A few more minutes and she might have been out of the clubhouse and on her way home, absolved from feeling any responsibility for the young victim. But she *had* been there when the emergency had been phoned through.

'There's a problem up on Ben Nevis,' Kirk had said grimly after answering his mobile phone. 'A young lad is stuck on a cliff. No one knows how he got there, but it seems he's hurt.'

Kirk had looked at her with sympathy in his eyes. 'There's no one else, Georgie,' he'd said quietly. He'd glanced at the clock on the wood-panelled wall. 'Damn it, I don't think the others are going to be back any time soon and I can't do much with this cursed wrist in a cast.'

Georgie had understood his frustration only too well. She'd

known her action-mad brother had been angry with himself for not wearing protective gear when he'd gone go-karting four weeks ago. Now his arm was encased in a cast from wrist to elbow, confining him to the clubhouse, manning the phone.

He held her gaze as he dialled the number of the mountain rescue team and asked for an update. His face fell as he listened to the reply. Snapping the phone shut, he turned to Georgie.

'They're at least another hour and a half away from getting back—and the weather's closing in. Damn, damn, damn.'

'I can climb to him, Kirk.' The words were out before she was aware she had been even thinking them. A little boy. Hurt. Alone. How could she not do something?

Kirk's gaze swept her face. 'Do you think that's a good idea? You haven't climbed for years.'

Georgie was already heading for the locker where her equipment was still stored. Kirk was right—she hadn't climbed for years—though force of habit ensured she kept everything in tip-top condition. 'It's not something you forget, Kirk. Of course I'll go,' she said quietly. 'There's no one else and I am a nurse. And a mother. If that were Jess…'

Kirk squeezed her shoulder. 'You don't have to do this. Nobody will think anything less of you, not after what you've been through.'

But *I* would, she thought. I'd think less of me—and it's me I have to live with. There was no way she could leave a child trapped, hurt and terrified on a ledge for any longer than was absolutely necessary. No matter what promises she had made to herself and to the memory of her dead husband.

She was already slipping into her harness. 'And that's why I'm going. I can't let anyone else go through what I did.'

Her brother regarded her steadily. Whatever he read in her eyes must have reassured him. 'Then I'm coming with you,' he said, gathering his gear together. Gone was his laconic teasing mood of earlier. In its place was focus and determination.

'What, with one arm?' Georgie said. 'Do you think that's a good idea?'

'Hey, me with one arm is still better than most men with two, sis. You know that.' He grinned but she could see he was already focussing on the climb ahead.

'Just as long as you don't think I'm back for good,' she said, deliberately keeping her tone light. She snapped her backpack closed. 'C'mon, slowcoach. Let's get going.'

It had taken half an hour of hard climbing to get where she was now. Luckily it was Kirk's left wrist that was broken and by a series of improvisations he was able to take the strain of her weight on the rope.

'I'm going to let myself slowly down beside you,' she called out to the frightened child. 'But first I'm going to drop a rope down. Tie it around your waist as best you can, okay?'

The boy nodded.

Georgie's arms ached with tension as she lowered herself carefully onto the ledge. Gingerly she tested her weight. Good. Although there was barely enough room for her and the child, it seemed stable enough.

Quickly she crouched beside him.

'What's your name?' she asked softly.

He didn't answer. Instead, his lip started quivering and tears rolled down his cheeks. He looked at her with abject misery. Georgie guessed panic was only moments away. She had to keep him calm until help arrived. She would have to do the talking for both of them.

'Well, I'm Georgie,' she began matter-of-factly. 'I'm a nurse and I used to work with Mountain Rescue. So I've done this kind of thing lots of time before.' *Lots of times before losing Ian, that was.* She hadn't been on a rescue mission since the accident and wouldn't be here now if she thought she'd any choice. Whatever nightmares she carried with her, she was doing what she had to do. Even if it meant doing the very thing she had promised herself she would never do again.

'I'm going to have a look at you then we're going to make a plan to get you off here,' she continued soothingly. 'You did the right thing by staying where you were, didn't you?' Georgie felt along his leg. Yup, broken, as she'd suspected, but at least the bone hadn't punctured the skin and she wasn't dealing with a compound fracture. That was something. Gently she removed the shoe on his injured leg and felt for the pulses in his foot.

'Can you feel me touching your toes?' she asked.

He sniffed and nodded. Good. Circulation and nerves intact. But did he have other injuries?

'Are you sore anywhere else? Any numbness or tingling— like pins and needles?'

The boy shook his head.

'Okay. I'm just going to lift your T-shirt and have a quick look at your tummy and chest.'

Superficially, at least, there was no sign of anything seriously wrong. So far, so good.

She pulled the pack off her back and removed the inflatable splint.

'I'm going to lift your leg and slip this underneath. It will hurt a bit, I'm afraid, but not for long, and once we have the splint inflated, your leg will feel a lot better.' As gently as she could she wrapped the boy's leg securely in the splint, his muffled cries of pain cutting into her heart.

When she'd finished, she gave him a quick hug. 'You're being very, very brave,' she told him. Spasmodic shudders racked the boy's body. It could be shock, pain or possibly internal injuries. Without proper equipment, her examination had been cursory at best. One way or another they needed to get him off the mountain and to a hospital. But how?

'Kirk?' she called into her radio. Her watch told her more than fifteen minutes had passed since she'd arrived on the ledge. It had only felt like a fraction of that time. 'Okay. I've had a quick look. GCS is fifteen, pulse about 100, breathing normal. No obvious injuries to chest, abdomen or spine. His tibia is broken—a clean break, luckily—and I've splinted the leg.'

Kirk would know that they couldn't be sure of anything until they could examine the child thoroughly and that the child needed to be taken to hospital as soon as possible. 'There's not a lot of room up here,' she continued, managing a reassuring smile at the youngster, who was watching her anxiously, 'but the ledge seems stable enough for now if we don't make any unnecessary movements.' She turned away and lowered her voice so that the boy couldn't hear. 'There's no way we'll be able to belay him off this ledge, though. It's too risky.'

'I'm ahead of you, sis,' Kirk replied. 'I've been in radio contact with RAF Gannet. They'll be with you in less than ten minutes and I've told them it's likely they're going to have to airlift him off the ledge. Oh, and can you ask the boy who was with him? I find it hard to believe he was on his own.'

'Copy that,' Georgie replied, relieved that the rescue helicopter wasn't far away. She should have known that Kirk would be on top of things. If he hadn't broken his wrist he'd be doing the rescue rather than co-ordinating things from the foot of the cliff.

'How're you holding up?' Kirk continued. Georgie could hear the concern in her brother's voice even through the crackle of the walkie-talkie. He knew how difficult this was for her. Not technically, but emotionally.

Carefully, Georgie settled herself down next to her charge, putting an arm around him for warmth and comfort. 'We're both doing fine,' she said, smiling down at the young boy. 'We'll sit tight and wait for the helicopter. I'll try and find out the answer to your questions in the meantime. So far I haven't even got a name. Speak later.'

The child, who had been listening to every word, started to cry in earnest. Georgie hugged his shoulders.

'Everything's going to be okay, I promise you. But we'll need to let your mum and dad know what's happened. Are you able to tell me your home number?' To her dismay, the young boy cried even louder; big gulping sobs of pain and distress.

'Hey,' Georgie reassured him. 'You're not in any trouble— they'll just be glad you're all right.'

Waiting for the helicopter to arrive, Georgie tried again to get some information from the little boy.

'Can you tell me your name?' she coaxed softly.

His eyes were solemn blue pools, etched with pain and fear. 'J-Jack,' he whispered as his sobs subsided.

Georgie smiled. 'Jack. That's a very nice name. Where do you live, Jack? Here in Fort William?'

Once more his lips trembled and his eyes filled, tears spilling over.

'It's not your fault,' Georgie consoled him hurriedly. 'Accidents happen all the time, even when we're careful.' She swallowed memories of Ian, her words sounding hollow even to herself. How many times had she tried to tell herself the same thing? And how many times had she wondered *if only*? She pushed the thoughts away. Thinking like that would drive her crazy. It certainly wouldn't bring her husband back.

The sound of a helicopter penetrated the still air and Georgie scanned the sky above. She squeezed Jack's hand. 'Not long now, sweetheart, until we get you out of here. And you'll certainly have a story to tell your pals when you see them.' The blades clattered loudly and the ground beneath them swirled with dirt as the downdraught from the aircraft battered the rock.

Georgie watched as a suited figure was lowered from the helicopter. In less than a minute he dropped, as light as a cat, onto the ledge beside them. He released himself from the rope and the helicopter swung away to a safe distance.

'Dr Logan Harris.' The man introduced himself with a slight gesture of his hand.

Relief came out in an explosion of breath. She hadn't expected a doctor. Normally the winchman was someone with first-aid knowledge, not a doctor. She had a brief impression of glinting brown eyes and even white teeth.

'What do we have? The mountain rescue guy told me you were a nurse.'

'A broken leg,' Georgie answered. 'I don't know if there are other injuries.'

Logan Harris yanked off his safety gloves with his teeth before crouching down to examine the boy, feeling across his ribs and abdomen.

'There's no obvious internal damage. He'll be checked out properly once we get him to hospital. Help me get him strapped into this harness.'

Logan turned to the boy. 'We'll have you off here and in hospital in a jiffy,' he said.

Working together in the cramped space, it only took a few minutes before Jack was securely fastened. Logan grinned his approval after he tested the last buckle. He spoke into his mike and the helicopter drew nearer.

'I'll take the lad up and come back for you in a second,' he shouted above the roar of the helicopter. The downdraught whipped her hair across her face and she struggled to keep it out of her eyes.

'It's okay. I can make it down myself,' she yelled back.

'Are you sure you don't want me to come back for you?' He reached out his hand for the line dropped by the helicopter and clipped it to the boy's harness.

For a moment there was nothing Georgie would have liked better. Although she had told Kirk that getting off the ledge would present no problem, that had been before the light had started to fade. It would be much trickier now. But the thought of getting into the helicopter caused her chest to tighten. She didn't want to go on an aircraft, not as long as she had a choice.

'No. It's okay. Honest. You get Jack to hospital. I'll be fine.'

As Logan finished preparing Jack for the ascent, the boy started to protest. 'M-Mum,' he said, panic lacing his voice.

Georgie had to put her ear to his mouth to catch the words. 'Don't worry, we'll get hold of your mum as soon as we get you off here,' she said.

'N-no.' The boy was having difficulty getting the words through his chattering teeth. 'Mum. She fell. Down there.' He pointed to Georgie's right and down the mountainside. She followed his finger but could see nothing. 'Mum was trying to get to me and she fell,' Jack persisted.

Georgie put a hand on the boy's shoulder. 'Where, Jack? Can you tell me exactly where she is?'

His face crumpled as fresh tears coursed down his cheeks. 'I don't know. I saw her coming towards me after I fell. Then she disappeared. I tried to phone her on my mobile, but she didn't answer. She's all right, isn't she?'

'Don't worry, we'll find your mum for you.' She relayed the information to Logan, who wouldn't have been able to hear the boy's words above the noise of the helicopter. 'He says his mother fell trying to reach him—we have no information about a female casualty. Have you?'

'No,' Logan replied, looking worried. 'We'll find out more when we get him out of here and somewhere safe.

'Let's get you into the helicopter and to the ambulance,' Logan said to the boy. 'Then the helicopter will have a look for her. Okay?'

He spoke into his mike and the helicopter moved until it was above them. The rotors whipped dust from the cliff side, forcing Georgie to bend her head against the dust that peppered her face. Logan turned to Georgie. 'We'll find the mother, don't worry. We'll be back as soon as we've dropped the lad.'

Logan and Jack were lifted up, and a sudden gust from the helicopter as it swung away almost made Georgie lose her tenuous grip. And she would have, if it hadn't been for the sudden increase in tension from the rope. Thank God she had managed to drive a bolt into the rock and thank God Kirk was keeping the rope taut. She and her brother had been climbing together all their lives and there was no one she would rather have protecting her back.

Then, without warning, a chunk of the crumbling cliff under her foot broke away and rolled down the mountainside. Georgie pressed herself against the rock face and held on for dear life.

Now she was really in trouble. Panic spiralled through her body.

Before she could move, another piece of rock broke away, and she only had about a foot of ledge left to stand on. She had to get off the crumbling ledge—and she had to do it quickly. But for the first time in her life she was rooted to the spot, frozen with fear. She didn't know if she could make her limbs respond to her commands.

Sorry, Ian. I know I promised myself I wouldn't do this any

*more—for our daughter's sake. But I didn't really have a
choice, did I?*

Thinking of her little girl gave her the strength she needed.
No way was her child going to lose two parents. Not while she
had breath left in her body. Testing the rope still attached to her
harness, Georgie forced her legs to move. *She was not going
to fall.* Kirk still had a firm grip of the other end of the rope.
There might yet be a danger that falling rocks from above could
tumble down and hit her, but she wouldn't think about that. She
couldn't abseil down for the same reason. Going higher
wouldn't work either. Above, there was only sheer rock face
and the rope she was using wasn't long enough. If she had more
time, she could ask Kirk to send up another rope and join that
one to the one she had. But time was a luxury she didn't have.
She had to move now. Staying where she was wasn't an option.

'I'm going move sideways and down to the next ledge,
Kirk,' she said into her radio. 'There's another casualty—the
mother. The helicopter is going to look for her as soon as they
drop the boy off.'

'Be careful, sis,' Kirk's voice crackled over the radio. He
didn't need to say any more. He, more than most, would know
exactly how dangerous the predicament she found herself in was.

Georgie eased herself over the side of the cliff. Don't think
about what can happen, she told herself. Think about something
else. Think about your daughter waiting for you at home.

Looking down, a wave of vertigo washed over her. It had
taken her precious minutes to travel less than a couple of feet
and the cliff she was reaching for was still some distance away.
Another rock tumbled from the ledge above, missing her head
by inches. Her heart sank as she realised she still couldn't risk
going down or up. All she could do was to keep on inching her
way to the side so she'd be away from the line of the falling

rocks. Then she would have to think again. Maybe Kirk would have a bright idea.

Taking a breath to try and quell the rising panic, she continued to move sideways, concentrating on finding footholds and places for her fingers to grip in the sheer rock.

Glancing to her left, she noted with relief that she had moved far enough away from the crumbling cliff and the falling rocks. Good. At the very least, if she could hang on, Kirk would find a way to get her off the damned mountain.

She looked up as the roar of the returning helicopter once again whipped dust into her face. Not that it would do her much good. The wind had picked up, and where she had moved to was under an overhang. There was no way the helicopter could get close enough to the mountainside to lift her off. No, it was down to her and Kirk. Although for the life of her, she couldn't see an easy way off the mountain.

Kirk came back on the radio. Perhaps he had a plan?

'Georgie, they're going to send someone down to get you off. Hold on there. They'll be with you in a tick.'

Georgie looked up to find the helicopter hovering dangerously close to the mountainside. Didn't they realise the danger?

'Tell them it's too risky,' she yelled back in to the radio. 'We'll have to think of something else.'

But to her astonishment a figure was already being lowered from the body of the aircraft. She held her breath as the figure swung perilously close to the rock face. Then he was beside her, still suspended. Dr Logan Harris. What kind of doctor was he? No other doctor she knew acted as winchman.

He held out a harness. The noise of the helicopter was too loud for her to make out what he was saying but the message was clear and there was no time to argue. The longer the helicopter stayed in the air, the greater the possibility of it crashing.

Georgie slipped the harness over her head. Then she was being gripped around her waist by strong legs. She unhitched herself from her rope and seconds later they were swaying in the wind as the helicopter lifted them up and swung them away from the mountain. Looking up, she found brown eyes glinting down at her. Unbelievably, he was grinning. If she hadn't known it was impossible, she would have swore he was enjoying himself.

A few terrifying minutes later and helping hands were reaching out, pulling them into the safety of the helicopter. For a moment, Georgie lay in a heap, just getting her breath. It wasn't as bad in the helicopter as she had feared. She couldn't see outside and she could *almost* make herself believe that they were on the ground.

'You okay?' Logan Harris was searching her face. 'You looked in real trouble there for a moment.'

Well, that was one way of putting it. If Logan Harris and the crew of the helicopter hadn't risked their lives to get her off the mountain, God only knew what would have happened. She hugged her legs to her chest as a wave of nausea washed over her. Now she was off the mountain, she couldn't stop shaking.

'By the way, this is Toby.' Logan indicated the man who had helped them on board. Toby flicked his finger at his helmet in a brief salute. 'We dropped Jack off at the bottom. The ambulance is going to take him to Fort William General. He'll be there by now.'

'What about Jack's mother?' She managed to force the words past numb lips.

Logan's radio buzzed and he listened intently. Then he and Toby moved to the open door and scanned the ground.

'What is it?' Georgie asked.

'A call just came in. The hospital's managed to get some more information from the boy. Apparently his mother's definitely still out here. No one has reported a woman looking for the boy.'

'She must be hurt. Probably unconscious. There is no way she wouldn't have noticed what was happening with her son otherwise. She would have phoned for help at the very least.'

Georgie glanced at her watch. 'It's been an hour since we got the call about the boy. That means the mother's been out there for at least that time.'

She and Logan looked at each other. If the mother had a head injury, time was critical. Georgie didn't want to think of the alternative.

Suddenly Toby pointed to something. Two figures on the ground were waving their jackets furiously. It could only mean one thing.

'I see her,' Logan said.

Georgie crept across to the open side of the helicopter. Once again a wave of vertigo slammed into her as she saw the ground far below. What was going on? This had never happened to her before. The thought of being in a small plane again nauseated her, but she'd hoped it would be different inside a helicopter. But there wasn't time to think about that now. The crewman was pointing to a flat piece of ground not far from where a body lay in a crumpled heap.

'We can land there,' he said, and spoke into his radio.

Mist was already covering the tops of the mountains, snaking ever closer to where the woman lay. Time was of the essence. If the mist got any thicker, visibility would make everyone's job much more difficult. It was even possible that the helicopter would have to leave and they'd have to attempt to get the victim to hospital on foot.

As soon as the helicopter touched down, Logan jumped out. Georgie ran after him, struggling to keep on her feet in the wind of the slowing rotors.

The climbers, a man and a woman, had stumbled across

the inert form a few moments earlier. It was a good thing they had, as Jack's mother must have fallen some distance and had come to rest almost underneath an enormous boulder. It was unlikely she would have been spotted from the air or that a rescue team on foot would have found her either. The passing climbers had covered her with jackets, but looked relieved to have help.

'I don't know what happened. I think she must have slipped on the scree and banged her head, but I can't be sure. I can see blood underneath her head, but we didn't want to move her,' the female climber told Georgie and Logan.

Georgie dropped to her knees beside Logan and the injured woman. Logan was checking her face. 'Her airway is fine and her breathing seems to be OK too,' he told Georgie.

'Hello,' she shouted into the woman's ear, while Logan was searching for a pulse. 'Can you hear me? My name's Georgie and I'm a nurse. There's a doctor here too. We're going to help you.'

There was no response. 'Pulse is weak and rapid.' Logan said. 'Can you check her level of consciousness?'

Georgie pressed the woman's fingernail firmly. She groaned softly and pulled her hand away slightly. Good. At least she was responding to pain.

A spreading red stain under the woman's head made it obvious that, whatever other injuries she had, she had taken a nasty blow to her skull and possible brain injury would be the main concern. Georgie slipped on gloves and felt around the back of the unconscious woman's head to feel the extent of the blow. Her fingertips came away sticky with blood, but it was hard to tell how badly she had cracked her skull.

Logan was feeling along the woman's chest and abdomen, checking for other injuries. 'Nothing obvious,' he said. Georgie knew that didn't mean that there wasn't something going on internally, though. Only a full examination at a hospital could verify that.

The unconscious woman groaned softly. Logan whipped out the small torch from the medical bag he carried with him and shone the light in her eyes. Although the pupils responded, the left pupil was bigger than the right.

The woman needed to get to hospital—and fast. Her initial head injury was bad enough but if there was more swelling inside the skull, the pressure would build up, causing permanent brain damage, possibly even death.

'Has she been conscious at all?' Georgie asked the climbers. They shook their heads. 'Not since we got here.'

Georgie put her mouth to the mother's ear. 'You're going to be all right,' she said, unsure whether the woman could hear her. 'Jack's okay. He's off the cliff and being checked over in hospital. But he's going to be fine.'

Without knowing more, Georgie knew they had to suspect a spinal injury. The sooner the woman was in a specialist unit the better. An A and E nurse she might be, but working in a well-equipped unit was entirely different from being outdoors in dying light in the wilds of Scotland with a woman who shouldn't be moved unnecessarily until a proper asessment had been made of her condition. Thank God there was a doctor with her who obviously knew what he was doing. It was a good thing too that the RAF helicopter was standing by. If it wasn't here, they'd be in much greater difficulty than they already were. She looked up to see Toby returning with a stretcher.

'We need to get this lady straight to the Glasgow City General's neurosurgery unit as quickly as possible. If we take her to the Fort William General she'll only have to be transferred to Glasgow later. It'll be risky lifting her onto a stretcher from here, but I don't think we have a choice.'

While Logan spoke he was fitting a neck brace. 'I can't tell at this stage whether there's a spinal injury. We'll have to immobilise her as best we can for the trip.'

By this time, Kirk had joined them. He gave his sister a quick hug then stood back to let them get on with seeing to the fallen woman. He must have realised that, with his broken wrist, he would only get in the way if he tried to help.

Quickly Georgie, Toby and Logan, with the help of the two passing climbers, slid the stretcher under the injured woman, taking care not to cause any unnecessary movement, and strapped her in place. Moments later, they were loading her into the helicopter.

'Do you want a lift?' Logan asked. Once again he grinned and a dimple appeared in his cheek. 'The weather's closing in and you must be exhausted.'

She summoned the biggest smile she could manage. Apart from having Jess waiting for her at home, the last thing she wanted was to go up in the helicopter again.

'The trip back down is a piece of cake,' she told Logan firmly. 'You just get Jack's mum to Glasgow and don't worry about me.'

Kirk stepped forward and placed his uninjured arm around Georgie's shoulders. 'She's right. Georgie is the last person you have to worry about on these mountains. She's like a cat,' he said. 'I'll make sure she gets down in one piece.'

Logan seemed doubtful. 'It's getting dark.' He jumped into the helicopter where Toby was securing the stretcher.

'Hey, Georgie and I could go down this mountain blind-folded. Couldn't we, sis?' Kirk said.

Logan glanced up at Kirk, obviously noting the family resemblance for the first time. While Kirk's hair wasn't nearly as red as hers, it had the merest hint of russet in its dark depths. Apart from that, Georgie knew she and her brother had almost identical eyes.

'I don't like it, but who am I to argue? You two obviously know what you're doing.' Then he grinned at Georgie and un-believably her heart did a crazy little dance in her chest. It was still beating rapidly as the helicopter lifted into the air, taking with it Dr Logan Harris.

'Good work, sis,' Kirk said once the helicopter had disappeared from view. 'Are you okay? It looked a little hairy back there.' He pulled her into his arms and hugged her tightly. 'It was a brave thing you did.'

Brave? Was it brave to do something when you had no choice? She had been terrified, but she had coped. She felt the old familiar surge of satisfaction. And, God, she had missed being out on the mountains, had missed being part of the mountain rescue team.

'Let's get out of here. I don't know about you, but I could do with a pint.' Kirk gave her a final squeeze before releasing her.

It wasn't a pint Georgie could do with. Quite frankly a magic wand to miracle her to the bottom of the mountain was what she needed. Now it was over, her legs had turned to jelly and she wondered if she could keep them working long enough to make the descent. She also knew that if she couldn't, Kirk was perfectly capable of carrying her down—plastered forearm or not—on his back if necessary. But she couldn't do that to him. One way or another she would have to force her mind away from the climb and the feelings it had brought flooding back and focus on something else. Like Logan Harris, for example, a little voice from nowhere chirped in her head. Think of him. Think of eyes the colour of the moor in winter and a fleeting grin that could stop a heart.

CHAPTER TWO

ONCE they were down, all Georgie wanted to do was collapse in a heap. And hug her daughter. But before she could do either, she wanted to go to the hospital and check on Jack. The little boy was bound to feel frightened and lonely, especially without a parent to comfort him. She also wanted to reassure him that his mother would be okay. If Jack were her son, she'd want someone to do the same.

But first she needed to phone her mother. Mary had come with her to Fort William for the two-week holiday and would have heard her children were involved with a rescue. She'd be worried sick and Georgie couldn't blame her. Ian hadn't been the only member of the mountain rescue team to have lost his life in recent years.

Sure enough, Mary's relief when she heard both her children were safely off the mountain was palpable.

'Are you all right?' she said anxiously. 'I mean, I know you're safe now, but it couldn't have been easy for you. Not after...' She didn't have to finish her sentence. Her mother knew she had sworn never to go on a rescue again and although she regretted the reasons for Georgie's decision, she had been grateful she would have one less child to worry about. If her mother had her way, Kirk would give up his position with the mountain rescue team too. Not that *that* was ever going to happen.

'I'm okay, Mum. I was just glad I was there to help. I kept thinking if it were Jess up there, alone and frightened.' She shivered. 'How would I have felt if no one had gone to help her? And that's why I want to go and check on Jack myself. They had to take his mum to a specialist unit in Glasgow, but he was taken to the Fort William General. He'll be alone, worried about his mum and bound to be shaky after his experience.'

'Of course you have to go and see him. Wee Jess is tucked up in bed fast asleep,' Mary said. 'She won't even know you're not home. I've kept supper for you and Kirk. It can go in the microwave when you get back.'

Trust Mum to be worried about their supper. She had never accepted that both her children were grown up and able to look after themselves. Except they weren't. At least she wasn't. After Ian's death, her mother had insisted on leaving her home here in Fort William and moving to Glasgow to help Georgie look after Jess. Her mother had given up her comfortable life without a thought so she could be with her daughter when she needed her, and had stayed. The only time her mother returned to her home town was when, as now, Georgie and Jess came too. Georgie was grateful. She'd never be able to work without her mother's help and support. Apart from Jess, work was what had got her through those terrible months following Ian's death.

But Georgie knew it was time she persuaded her mother that she could cope on her own. Jess had just been offered a place at nursery, starting in the autumn. With Jess at nursery full time, Mary was no longer needed as much to help with the child care. Although she would miss her mother terribly, she had to persuade her to come back here where all her friends and interests were. Georgie smiled. Kirk would become the full focus of Mary's attention for a change. Although he loved their mother dearly, she was always going on at him to find a good woman and settle down. And Kirk wasn't a settling-down kind of guy.

It took her another hour before she was able to leave the clubhouse. The rest of the team, who had returned from their rescue, were full of questions and refused to let her go until she had given them a blow-by-blow account. Like Kirk, they knew she hadn't been out on a rescue since Ian had died and were concerned and anxious to hear how she had coped.

'I'm okay,' she reassured them. 'It got a bit dodgy, but it all turned out okay.'

She couldn't bring herself to tell them about the few minutes when she'd been terror-stricken and unable to move.

'Does that mean you're back with the team, Red?' Mike, one of the guys she had climbed with many times before, asked.

'No, Mike. Remember I live in Glasgow now? So it's hardly going to happen.'

But apart from the fear, she *had* felt exhilarated—once it was all over. In many ways she had missed the companionship of the team as well as the adrenaline rush of climbing. But, she reminded herself, that life was finished. She had a daughter who needed a mother to be around for a very long time to come.

All in all it had been a couple of hours since the helicopter had left with Jack's mother. By now there should be news of how she was doing. Perhaps the nurses at the Fort William General would have heard? Leaving Kirk and the rest of the guys, who were planning to move on to their usual watering hole, Georgie jumped into her small car and headed for the hospital, her mind still inexplicably filled with images of a dark-eyed man with a heart-stopping grin.

* * *

Georgie knew the staff at the Fort William General well. After all, she had worked with them for six years before moving to Glasgow. Whenever she was visiting Kirk in Fort William, she always dropped in for a cup of coffee.

Lindsay was on duty in A and E and after a brief hug and a disappointed look over her shoulder—she had always carried a torch for Kirk—led her to the cubicle where Jack was in the process of having his broken leg put in a cast. Jack looked up and his face broke into a smile. But it was the man sitting next to him playing on a games console who stopped her breath. Logan Harris! What on earth was he doing here? It was almost as if thinking about him had made him appear. He had peeled down his flying suit to his waist, revealing a hard, taut chest and powerfully muscled arms under his T-shirt.

Behind him, Lindsay wiggled her eyebrows questioningly and grinned. Like everyone else who knew about Ian, she was always telling Georgie it was time to date again.

'Have a coffee with me if you have time?' Lindsay said before she disappeared.

Logan got to his feet and held out his hand. 'I just came to tell Jack about his mum,' he said. 'But I'm pleased to meet you properly.' He shot another devastating smile in her direction and Georgie almost reeled from the force of it. Without his helmet she could see him properly, and if it were possible he was even more attractive than she had thought at first. Although not conventionally good-looking—his features were too rugged for a start—he had a charisma and easy confidence about him that suggested he was used to women finding him attractive. His hair was cropped short, military style, and his face was sculpted over high cheekbones. Only a scar, running from just underneath his cheekbone to the corner of his mouth, marred his good looks, but in some obscure way it only made him more attrac tive in Georgie's eyes. Add a six-foot-something frame and a dose of sex appeal Georgie had only ever associated with film stars and it all added up to a mind-blowing package. All of this didn't tie in with a man who would take the time out to stay with a frightened boy. Georgie was intrigued. And how on earth had he got back here from Glasgow? If he'd driven he must have raced along the roads at breakneck speed.

Long fingers grasped her hand in a firm grip, and sparks shot up Georgie's arms.

'Georgie McArthur,' she said faintly. She dragged her eyes away from him and turned to Jack.

'Hey. How're you doing?'

'Dr Harris says Mum's awake, but still in Intensive Care in Glasgow. He says she's going to have to stay in hospital for a day or two, but she's going to be okay.'

The terrified little boy of earlier was gone. Now he knew his mum was going to be all right, excitement had taken over.

'What about your dad?' Georgie asked. 'Wasn't he with you?' The light went out of Jack's eyes.

'He lives in Edinburgh. Mum and him aren't living together right now. They say they're having a little break from each other. But I don't believe them. I think they're getting a divorce. Mum's been crying all the time. I made her come up here to try and get her mind off it and look what happened. If I hadn't done what she told me not to, she wouldn't have tried to come after me and fallen.' His lips trembled as he remembered his terror.

'Hey,' Georgie said soothingly, 'accidents happen. Your mum will be proud of how brave you were—I promise.'

'Anyway, Dad's with her now. He came from Edinburgh as soon as he heard she was hurt. He can't come and see me 'cos he doesn't want to leave Mum on her own.'

Georgie read the hope in his eyes. It didn't take a mind reader to know his nine-year-old mind already had his parents back together. Georgie prayed he wasn't going to be disappointed.

'The hospital says I have to stay in tonight. But Dr Harris says he's going back to Glasgow tomorrow, so he'll go with me in the ambulance car if I want.'

Georgie shot a surprised look at Logan. Surely such thoughtfulness was beyond what was required?

'His mum was taken directly to the head injuries unit at Glasgow City. It seemed sensible. If we'd stopped here and she'd ended up having to be transferred there anyway...' He lifted an eyebrow slightly, not wanting to complete the sentence in front of Jack.

'I really, really want to see my mum—and dad.' Jack's lip trembled and Georgie's heart went out to him. She knew he wouldn't believe his mum was okay until he saw her for himself.

Georgie smiled reassuringly. 'The Glasgow City just happens to be the best hospital in Scotland for people who have hurt their heads,' she said. 'I work there. So I know your mum is in very good hands.'

Logan looked surprised. 'You do? Work there, I mean?' He eyed her speculatively. 'I assumed you were a nurse here.'

'I used to be, until a few years ago. I'm just here on holiday. I'd take Jack myself but I'm not going back to Glasgow until Sunday night.'

'I've got to go back there tomorrow anyway,' Logan continued. 'So it makes sense for me to go with Jack. It would save his father from making the three-hundred-mile round trip. I spoke to him on the phone and he's relieved to have that taken care of.'

'Don't you have to go back with your crew?' she asked. 'To HMS Gannet? Isn't that where the RAF is based? Aren't you with them?' A sticker on his T-shirt bore the name Major Harris.

'I'm not actually with the RAF. I just happened to be visiting their base when the call came through and I was happy to volunteer my services.'

'So how come you're here? Didn't you go with Jack's mother to the Glasgow City General?'

'We were heading in that direction when the Fort William General radioed to let us know they had a visiting neurologist from Glasgow who was spending the day teaching some junior doctors here. It made more sense for her to go with Jack's mother and there are people I need to talk to here. So the helicopter picked her up and dropped me off. She phoned a few minutes ago to give us an update. That's how we know she's doing okay.' He winked at Jack.

Georgie was more and more curious. She waited for him to continue.

'And, since you are obviously interested, it so happens that the Glasgow City General is going to be my home for the next three months.'

Georgie's cheeks grew warm. It was a Highland habit she hadn't ever really managed to lose—this interest in other people. City people thought it was nosy to ask questions, Highlanders knew it was only polite interest—or at least that's what they told themselves and each other.

Logan slid her a look and the wheels clicked into place. There had been talk in the A and E department of a consultant from one of the forces coming on loan for three months to look into setting up an emergency medical retrieval team similar to the one the army had perfected. Could it be this man? Georgie had expected someone a lot older for some reason. Someone closer to retirement age. Not this hunk.

'Are you the doctor who is coming to set up the new emergency service?' she asked bluntly, ignoring the way her heart was doing a little dance behind her ribs.

'Got it in one.' He moved his hand in a mock salute. 'Major Harris at your service. How did you know?'

'As one of the A and E nurses at the Glasgow City General, I'd heard the rumours, but I don't make it to the inter-departmental meetings as often as I should so I've only gathered bits and pieces.' She blew out her cheeks. 'I've been on holiday here for the last couple of weeks, so I must have missed the latest.'

He grinned back and her heart did that complicated ma-noeuvre inside her chest again. 'I'll be there on Monday,' he said. 'I've a bit of information gathering still to do, including forming links with the other emergency services in the area. Which reminds me, I don't suppose you have a number where I can get hold of the mountain rescue team leader, do you?'

She raised an eyebrow.

'We'll be working with them at some point, so I want to talk to them. I might as well do it now, seeing as I'm here for the night. No point in wasting an opportunity.'

Georgie thought for a moment. Jess would be fast asleep and likely to remain so for the remainder of the night. Kirk and the rest of the team would still be hanging out at the inn where they met most evenings to dissect the day's climbing and the rescue. She could just give Logan Kirk's telephone number and leave him to make his own arrangements. But that would be churlish. She made up her mind.

'You met the team leader earlier—my brother Kirk. I can give you a lift to where he and the rest of the team will be, if you like.'

He smiled broadly. 'I was hoping you'd say that.'

Georgie and Logan left Jack, who had dozed off while they'd been speaking. Georgie breathed a sigh of relief when she saw Lindsay was no longer outside in the A and E area. She must have gone for her break, which was just as well. Georgie knew her ex-colleague's curiosity would have known no bounds had she seen her leave with Logan.

Outside, Georgie watched in amusement as Logan folded his long legs with difficulty into the passenger seat of her Mini. Even with the seat pushed back to its furthest position, he still looked cramped.

The last of the sun had disappeared from the sky when they set off from the hospital, the full moon the only light on the dark road.

'The inn is a few miles out of Fort William,' she explained. 'At the foot of the mountains. All the climbers meet there to analyse the day's climbing and plan their next climb. After that they relax with a pint or two and maybe some music.'

'Does the inn have rooms?'

'Yes, but it's a holiday weekend, so I'm afraid it's likely to be booked up. Loads of people travel up at this time of the year to climb the mountains. Some come from as far away as London, or Europe.' The implication of what he was asking hit her. 'Of course, you don't have anywhere to stay, do you?'

''Fraid not. I didn't expect to find myself here, let alone staying the night. I don't even have a toothbrush with me. I assumed it would be easy enough to get a room somewhere.'

She hesitated. What she was about to suggest was making her feel like a teenager asking someone out on a first date, which was ridiculous. It was simply the polite thing to do. 'Then you'll just have to stay the night at our house. There's plenty of space. And it will mean you and Kirk will get a chance to talk without interruptions.'

'He's staying with you?'

'Actually, we're staying with him. My mum's there too and my daughter, but there's still a room free.'

She glanced across at him. Even in the dark she could see his eyes drop to her left hand where she still wore her wedding ring.

'And your husband? Did you leave him behind in Glasgow?'

'I'm a widow,' she said shortly, hearing the hitch in her voice. Saying the words still brought a lump to her throat.

'I'm sorry,' Logan said.

Silence stretched between them. This was the part when *she* usually got twenty questions. But thankfully Logan didn't ask any more. Either he thought it was none of his business or he could tell from her voice that she didn't want to talk about it.

'Thanks for the offer of a room,' he said finally, 'but I couldn't put you out. I'm used to making do wherever I can find a bed. I'm sure I can persuade the inn to squeeze me in somewhere. Even if it's in a hut outside.'

Georgie shook her head. 'Nope. Sorry. Highland hospitality won't allow it. There is no way my mother would forgive me if I let you fend for yourself.'

'If you're sure—great. Thank you.'

'That's settled, then. I'll phone Mum once I've dropped you and ask her to make up the spare room.' Although Georgie kept her voice matter-of-fact, her heart was doing its little dance again.

'Where do you call home?' Georgie asked. 'I can't place your accent.' Damn. Here she was doing the question thing again, just when she'd promised herself she wouldn't. But she couldn't help it—she was intensely curious about this enigmatic man.

'People tell me I don't really have an accent. Probably because I've travelled all over.' A shadow crossed his face, to be replaced seconds later by an easy grin. 'That tends to happen when you're a regular with the army.'

'But there must be somewhere you call home!'

'I've rented a place in Glasgow for three months, simply because I didn't fancy staying in a hotel for that long. It's the first time in years that I've stayed for that amount of time in one place. So I guess it's home for the time being.'

Georgie felt a pang of sympathy. Her dad had been in the army before he'd retired. She had hated being moved from pillar to post, never really having time to make friends or settle down before moving on. The first time she had ever had somewhere to call home had been when her father had taken early retirement and moved the family to Fort William where *his* parents had lived all their lives. The last few years of Georgie's childhood had been spent somewhere settled and she had thrived. Since then, Georgie's life had been rooted in Scotland and her family and she could think of nothing worse than not having a place to call home. If it hadn't been for the support of family and friends after Ian had died, she'd never have been able to cope.

'And your family?'

It was as if the shutters had come down. The atmosphere in the car turned decidedly cool.

'The army is my family,' he said briefly. His mouth curved in to a half-smile. 'Anyway, I'd rather talk about you.'

Some pair they made. He didn't want to talk about his life and she didn't want to talk about hers.

However, she couldn't help wondering what he wasn't telling her.

The road was rising steeply but Georgie knew the West Coast like the back of her hands. She could almost have navigated them in her sleep. The mountains of Glencoe rose like cloaked giants on either side of the road. She never failed to feel the brooding loneliness of the place where the Campbells had massacred the MacDonalds.

'Have you always climbed?' Logan asked.

'Since like for ever. My father took me out on the hills as soon as I could walk. If I got tired, he'd fling me like a rucksack on his back.' Georgie smiled at the memory, before the familiar tug of grief pulled at her heart. Although her father had died four years ago, she still missed him. 'I was brought up here. I've climbed every hill in Scotland, including the Munros, at least twice. I joined the mountain rescue team when I was eighteen. Unfortunately tourists and even experienced climbers constantly underestimate our mountains—especially how quickly the weather can change. I've even seen women set off in their high heels for a four-hour climb. And then they're surprised when they twist their ankle and have to be rescued. I also volunteer as a rescue medic at the annual downhill cycle race that's held in Fort William every year.'

'But you live in Glasgow now?'

'Yes. And have done for the last two and a half years. I'm not really part of the mountain rescue team any more. Today was unusual. I just happened to be hanging out at the clubhouse with Kirk when the call came through. The team was out on another call, so I said I would go.' She took a shaky breath, remembering how she had frozen and the vertigo she'd experienced. It had never happened before, but this had been the first time she'd climbed since before Jess had been born. Just as well, then, that she was no longer part of the team.

Georgie felt Logan's eyes on her and when she glanced his way he was looking thoughtful.

'What's the most difficult rescue you've been involved with?'

His question was unexpected and hit her right in the solar plexus. She couldn't bear to think about the most difficult rescue. She had spent the last two and a half years trying not to think about it.

'Georgie?' Logan prompted. Her silence must have told him she didn't want to talk about it. 'It's okay,' he said 'You don't have to tell me. God knows, there's stuff I don't want to talk about.'

So she was right. There was a lot more to Logan Harris than met the eye. He puzzled her. On the one hand, he seemed to be a typical all-male action man—on the other, he had this surprising thoughtfulness. He had cared enough to go and see Jack, knowing the child would be frightened and anxious.

She didn't know whether she was relieved or disappointed when the lights of the inn broke through the darkness.

'We're here. I'll make the introductions and then get away and help Mum with the spare room.' Right now all she wanted was to be away from this man's searching eyes—and his questions.

'Are you sure you don't want me to at least ask about a room here? Maybe I'd be lucky.'

'Honestly, there's no problem. Whatever you prefer. If there isn't space or you just change your mind about asking, Kirk will bring you back with him. Actually, come to think of it, he'll probably insist on it. You can drive his car, otherwise, knowing my brother, he'll be tempted to drive himself—even with one arm in plaster. And he drives like a madman at the best of times.'

'Seems like you and your brother are one of a kind—you both enjoy putting your lives in danger,' Logan said, and Georgie couldn't tell whether it was approval or the opposite in his voice.

Little did he know that he had got it completely wrong. Kirk might still love pitting himself against the mountain, and she might have done once, but all she wanted these days was an easy life. A safe, uncomplicated life for her and Jess.

Inside, the inn was a cacophony of sound. Someone had brought out an accordion and Kirk had retrieved his fiddle from behind the bar and in his typical nothing-is-going to-stop-me-doing-what-I-want way had tucked the instrument under his plastered left arm while he played the strings with his right. When he spotted them he waved.

'Trust Kirk not to miss a chance to play the fiddle.' Georgie indicated her brother with a nod of her head. 'He'll be over as soon as he finishes the set.'

'Hey, Red.' A stocky man with a woollen hat rushed to their side. 'I didn't expect to see you here.'

Logan mouthed '*Red?*' at her with a broad grin on his face. Georgie wished Rob and the rest would get over using the nickname they had given her when she'd been a teenager and had first started hanging out with them.

'Rob, this is Dr Logan Harris. He wanted to meet you guys and to speak to Kirk in particular. I need to get home. Would you mind telling Kirk that Logan would like a word when he's free? And tell him Logan will be staying the night at the house?'

'Sure thing, Red. Hey, how's that wee kiddie of yours? Kirk's always telling us she's the spitting image of Ian.'

'Will you stop calling me Red?' Georgie muttered in his ear, before straightening. 'Jess is fine. Growing fast. I brought her in the other day, but I gather you were up some mountain—as usual. I'm away back to Glasgow tomorrow night, so you'll have to wait until next time, I'm afraid.'

Once more she was conscious of Logan's eyes on hers. Unable to help herself, she slid him a glance. He was looking at her wedding ring.

'The guys will look after you. I'll see you later, Logan,' she said, and quickly made her escape.

As she drove home Georgie couldn't stop thinking about Logan. He was coming to work at the Glasgow City Hospital! And he would be working in the same department as her too! Or would he? The chat about the doctor coming to set up the new service hadn't been terribly specific as to where he'd be based, but he was bound to be in the department some of the time at least. For some crazy reason her heart started doing its little dance at the thought. Stop it! she told herself angrily. You don't know the first thing about him. Except that he is sexy as hell. And not just mildly attractive either. More like blowing-your-socks-off, drop-dead gorgeous!

The realisation hit her like a ton of bricks. It was the first time she had even thought about another man, let alone found one attractive. A shock of guilt and dismay shot through her. How could she even think of another man when she had loved Ian so much? Eventually, sometime—in the year dot maybe—she would have to move on with her life. People had told her time would heal, that eventually her heart would mend, but she hadn't believed them. If that meant forgetting about Ian, she didn't know if she wanted her heart to heal. Forgetting about him, her first love, the father of her child, seemed so disloyal. What *was* she thinking? She could no more forget Ian than fly to the moon. But some easing of the pain that had almost crushed her had to be good.

She shook her head. All this turmoil just because she had met a man who made her pulse race. She didn't even know if he was married. Someone as gorgeous as him was bound to be. Besides, the look in his eyes, the excitement, the thrill of danger. She had seen that look before. In Ian's eyes.

Married or not, Georgie thought impatiently, Dr Logan Harris was not for her.

'And you say you're going to be working with this man?' Mary asked as they made up the bed in the spare room. 'What's he like?'

Kirk had telephoned to say that the inn was full and Logan was taking up Georgie's offer of a bed for the night.

'Oh, you know. Tall,' she replied evasively. Her mother was also always telling her it was time to move on. Georgie knew as soon as Mary saw Logan she'd start imagining all sorts of scenarios. All sorts of never-going-to-happen scenarios. 'Anyway, you'll meet him yourself. If not tonight, at breakfast tomorrow.'

'And he's an army doctor?' Mary persisted. 'What's he going to be doing in Glasgow, then?'

'Setting up a medical emergency retrieval service. He's only there for three months—or so I understand.'

'Is he young?'

'Thirty-something at a guess. C'mon, Mum. I know what's going through your mind. But forget it. He might be married for all I know. And, anyway, I don't want a relationship with another man.' She twisted her wedding ring. 'I still miss Ian, Mum.'

This time she couldn't help the catch in her voice. Her mother stopped what she was doing and came over and hugged her. 'Ian would want you to move on with your life, you know. All he ever wanted was your happiness. You can't mourn him for ever.'

'I know that. I guess I'm just not ready yet. Besides…'

'Go on,' Mary prompted.

'Besides, even if I were, I could never fall for someone who puts his life in danger on a daily basis. Not after what happened to Ian. If I do meet someone else, believe me, it's going to be someone whose idea of a wild night is watching an action movie on the telly.'

'I can't imagine you being happy with that sort of man. You've always craved excitement.'

'Honestly, Mum. I've had enough excitement to last me a lifetime. All I want now is to make a home for me and Jess. Somewhere secure for both of us.' She looked at Mary, noticing, not for the first time, that her mother was getting old. Despite her protestations, Georgie could tell the arthritis in her left hip was getting worse. 'It's time we let you get back to your own life. You've put it on hold for long enough.'

'That's not what I meant when I said it's time for you to get over your grief,' Mary protested. 'You know I love looking after Jess. It's you I'm worried about.'

'I couldn't have managed these last two and a half years without you, you know that. But, as you say, it's time I stood on my own two feet. And part of that means letting you get back to your home. You can't tell me that you don't miss it.'

'A house—a place—is nothing compared to being with those you love when they need you. And you still need me. I'll stay as long as you need me, *mo ghràigh*,' her mother said quietly. 'You know that, don't you?'

When Georgie woke up the next morning she was astonished to find it was after eight. She had fallen into bed soon after they'd finished getting the spare room ready and had gone out like a light. Probably something to do with yesterday's unaccustomed exercise.

Throwing the bedclothes aside, she sprang out of bed. Normally Jess would have woken her long before now, jumping on the bed or crawling in beside her for a story, but the house was ominously quiet. She rushed to Jess's room. It was empty. Where was she? Mary was going out for the day and had obviously gone already, so Jess couldn't be with her. Kirk would have left for the hospital ages ago. Georgie was beginning to panic. Could Jess have let herself out of the house? What if she had wandered into the street? Or to the stream that flowed near the house?

Heart in mouth, Georgie charged into the kitchen and stopped dead in her tracks. Jess was sitting at the table next to a bemused Logan, chatting away. In her panic Georgie had completely forgotten he had spent the night. She hadn't heard him and Kirk come in.

Her daughter's plump, toddler cheeks were flushed pink and her hair was a tangle of curls around her face. She looked, as usual, adorable. 'Jess,' Georgie breathed, almost dizzy with relief.

'Mummy!' Jess cried happily when she saw Georgie. 'Uncle Logan's been reading to me.'

Uncle Logan? Where had *that* come from? Jess was usually shy with strangers.

Amused, slightly stunned brown eyes found hers. 'She toddled into the kitchen before Kirk left, wanting a story read to her, so I was happy to oblige. We enjoyed "The Enormous Crocodile" *twice* and before that we watched a DVD about some strange teddy bears with holes in their stomachs—um, let me see, three times, or was it four?'

Poor Logan. He obviously hadn't a clue that there was nothing Jess liked more than undivided attention. And equally obviously he had never been confronted with the Teletubbies either!

'You should have sent Jess in to me,' she remonstrated softly, feeling slightly guilty. 'I'm usually up by now. I don't know how I managed to sleep through my alarm…'

'Your mother wanted to wake you, but I said to let you sleep as long as possible.'

'Oh! How long have you been up?'

'Since six. Don't worry, that's my usual time.' Logan grinned, his eyes creasing at the corners, and Georgie's heart tumbled. His eyes travelled across her body and she blushed as she realised she was only wearing pyjama bottoms and a very skimpy top. Hastily, she retreated out of the kitchen.

'I'll just get dressed. Then I'll make us some breakfast,' she said over her shoulder.

'Take your time, Jess and I have had porridge oats already,' came the amused reply. 'And I think there are still several books in Jess's pile.'

After a hasty shower and a too-long dither over what to wear, Georgie settled on black jeans and a moss-green V-neck jersey before returning to the kitchen. Logan and Jess were still at the table looking at books, but Georgie was sure his eyes were beginning to glaze over. There was, after all, only so much of books for a three-year-old anyone, except a parent, could take. Thinking of which, she still didn't know whether he was married and had children. Someone this comfortable with a three-year-old was bound to have his own. Dismayed at the stab of disappointment she felt at the thought, Georgie picked Jess up and squeezed her tight.

'I think we'd better give *Uncle Logan…*' she slid a pointed look in his direction '…a little break, don't you?'

Jess was bubbling over with excitement 'He's been telling me about the 'copter he flies and he says he's going to work in your hospital, Mummy. Is that true? Can he live with us and Granny in Glasgow?'

'Logan will want to stay in his own house, *mo ghaol*. Now, off you go and get dressed. Call me if you need help.' The thought of Logan living with them was sending all sorts of unwanted fantasies fizzing around her brain.

Georgie placed her daughter back on her feet and gently prodded her in the direction of her bedroom. Jess, with a great show of reluctance, left them alone.

'Speaking of which, where is the flat you've rented in Glasgow?' Georgie asked politely.

'On the Clyde, overlooking the river. It's small but has everything I need. Down to the latest music system. It's also handy for the hospital.'

'And will your family be joining you?' Georgie asked, curiosity getting the better of her.

As he quirked an eyebrow in her direction she added hastily, 'You seem so comfortable with Jess I thought you must be used to kids.' The words were out before she could stop them.

Logan grinned ruefully. 'Nope. No wife. No nephews, no nieces. Or brothers or sisters.'

'What, none at all? What about your parents?' She was doing it again. Opening her mouth before she had engaged her brain.

Once again a strange look crossed Logan's features.

'They're dead. When I was a kid,' he said shortly.

Georgie could have bitten her tongue. She had gone in there with two big feet. How terrible to grow up without parents. It really was time she learned when to keep her mouth shut.

Before she could apologise, Logan held up a hand. 'Would you mind if we changed the subject?' Although his voice was light, there was a tightness around his mouth that told Georgie he was hurting.

Georgie switched on the kettle, glad that she had her back to him so that he wouldn't see her confusion—or her pity. She knew instinctively that Logan would hate sympathy. But someone must have brought him up. An aunt perhaps? Grandparents? Why, then, the reference to the army being his family? She wanted to know more. She wanted to know everything about this man. And he wasn't married. That shouldn't make a difference to her but it did. She was burning with curiosity, but his expression made it clear that the subject was closed. At least for now.

'Coffee?' she asked.

Logan shook his head.

'I think it's time I went to the hospital to collect Jack. I'm sure he's desperate to see his folks.' He was no longer the smiling, relaxed man of earlier. His voice was stiff and his eyes hooded. It seemed her open curiosity had upset or annoyed him.

There was nothing for it but to call the taxi for him, and they waited for the few minutes it took to arrive in uncomfortable silence. When the taxi tooted its arrival, Logan stood and held out his hand. Still bewildered, Georgie shook it.

'Please thank your mother for me—and Kirk. Tell him the information he gave me will be invaluable.' Just then Jess appeared at the doorway, dressed in a bizarre combination of dress and shorts. Despite the tension in the room, Georgie had to smile. It was typical of her daughter. If she couldn't choose what to wear, she simply wore everything she fancied.

Jess ran up to Logan and flung her arms around his legs.

'Are you coming back?' she asked, tilting her head up to read his expression.

Logan crouched down beside her, his face relaxing into a smile. 'Maybe,' he said. 'But perhaps I'll see you in Glasgow? I'll certainly be seeing your mum there.' He turned to Georgie, looking as if he was about to say something. But when the taxi gave another impatient toot of its horn, Logan sketched a wave and left them alone.

In the taxi, Logan sank back against the seat, his mind filled with images of Georgie. Her red curls, framing a delicate face; her impish smile that couldn't quite disguise the sadness in her grey eyes. He thought about the lie he had told her. It was one he was used to telling when anyone asked, but it didn't make him feel any better—although his parents might as well be dead. Over the years he had said it so often, sometimes he almost believed it. What was the alternative? Telling people that his mother had abandoned him to the care system when he was just two years old—younger than Jess. It had been bad enough when he'd been a child in school. His teachers had treated him differently when they'd known he was in care. They'd expected him to show behavioural problems—and so he had. He'd kept getting into trouble. Nothing too serious—a broken window, playing truant—but it had been enough to convince his teachers he had no future. If it hadn't been for the army cadet programme one of his care workers had suggested, he probably would have lived up to everyone's expectations and amounted to nothing. But the discipline of army life had suited him. He had buckled down at school and made something of his life. If his teachers knew he had made it through medical school, they wouldn't believe it. He owed the army big-time.

But Georgie was different. He didn't know how he knew it, he just did. Maybe it was the way she looked at him, with her steady, honest eyes. Although he barely knew her, he knew instinctively she would never judge him. Just as he knew that she would never in a millions years give up her child. Whatever happened in her life, she'd fight tooth and nail for her daughter.

She was the most intriguing woman he had met for a long time—feisty and caring at the same time. She had welcomed him into her family home without a second thought and he had betrayed that trust with a lie. Although he hardly knew her, he couldn't imagine *her* lying to save her life.

Despite the warm manner and calm eyes, there were faint lines around her eyes, lines that spoke of pain. The lines, however, didn't make her any less beautiful. If anything, they made her strong features and full mouth even more appealing. She was a heady mixture of vulnerability and strength and he'd never met anyone like her. What had happened to Jess's father? Georgie was still wearing her wedding ring. As usual, it was the first thing he checked out when he met a woman he found attractive.

The thought brought him snapping to attention. Hey, don't go there. She wasn't his type. Even though he hardly knew her, it was obvious Georgie wasn't the love-me-and-leave-me type of woman. And there was the matter of the dead husband. Widows were even more off-limits than married women. He liked his relationships uncomplicated and temporary, and something in his blood told him Georgie was neither.

He sank back in his seat. Hell, he had three months. Plenty of time to find out more about Georgie McArthur, and thinking about what he was going to do about her was much more interesting than his own problems.

CHAPTER THREE

ON Monday morning, Georgie was back in Glasgow and ready to return to work. She left the house earlier than usual, wanting a few extra minutes so she could check up on Jack's mum. When she arrived at the hospital, she went straight to the neurology ward. If Jack's mother was still in hospital, this was where she'd find her.

And, sure enough, in the first single room, sitting up in bed with Jack beside her was the woman from the mountain. Apart from the bandage around her head and a nasty bruise on her cheekbone, she looked as if she was recovering well.

As soon as Jack noticed Georgie in the doorway, he picked up his crutches and with remarkable dexterity hopped towards her.

'Hey, Mum. This is Georgie,' he said. 'You know, the lady from the mountains. The one that helped you and rescued me.'

Georgie felt her cheeks grow hot. 'I think that's a bit of an exaggeration, Jack. I wasn't the only one involved. There was a whole team of us, in fact—including the RAF.'

'I told her about the helicopter and the winch. It was so cool. Almost worth breaking my leg for,' Jack said excitedly. 'But if you hadn't come onto the ledge, I could have fallen before the helicopter came back for me.'

Georgie shrugged her shoulders. It was clear Jack had his own version of events and was sticking to them.

'Thank you so much for everything you did,' the woman in the bed said softly, her eyes damp. 'If it hadn't been for you, I don't know what might have happened.' She flicked her eyes in the direction of her son.

'We were lucky that the RAF could help. You're not the first to get in trouble in the mountains and I dare say you won't be the last.'

Just then a man appeared, pausing in the doorway as if uncertain of his welcome.

'This is my dad, Georgie,' Jack said, his eyes shining. 'He's been here all the time since they brought Mum in. And he says he's coming back to live with us. Isn't that right, Dad?'

The man crossed over to the bed, took his wife's hand in his, and smiled down at her. Georgie could tell that, whatever had been wrong with this couple's marriage, they still loved each other deeply. Sometimes it took a near tragedy to bring people to their senses. Georgie had seen it before. Happily, it seemed as if Jack's optimism back on the ledge had been well founded.

'This is my husband, Steve, and I'm Caroline,' Jack's mother said. 'It seems crazy that I didn't even know your name until Jack told me.'

'So you're Georgie,' Steve said, pumping Georgie's hand. 'I can't thank you enough for bringing my wife and son safely back to me.' As he turned to look deep into his wife's eyes, Georgie knew he wasn't simply talking about the rescue. She swallowed the lump in her throat. So often in A and E, they didn't get the chance to follow up on their patients. This was a rare pleasure.

The sound of a cough behind her made her whirl round. Logan was standing in the doorway, holding a bunch of comics.

'I see Nurse McArthur has beaten me to it,' he said in his deep, almost accent-free voice. 'The nurses told me they plan to discharge you later today so I just wanted to check up on you myself.'

He wasn't in uniform. And he'd shaved. Dressed in a tailored suit with a blindingly white shirt, he looked different, less approachable than the day they'd met and Georgie felt inexplicably tongue-tied.

'I'd better get down to the department,' she said hastily. 'My shift's due to start.' She made a show of looking at her watch. 'Oh, in about five minutes. I'm really glad that you're all doing so well. It makes everything worthwhile.' And before anyone could stop her she was charging back down the stairs as if she was being chased by demons. Which, in a way, she guessed she was.

The A and E department was already busy, although it wasn't quite eight. After changing into her uniform of trousers and tunic, Georgie made her way to the staffroom where the ward report would be about to start. Inside she found Lata, one of her colleagues, studying the board where all the patients were written up.

'Hi, Georgie. Good holiday?' she asked.

Lata, with coffee-coloured skin and almond-shaped eyes, was naturally reserved but she had a mischievous sense of humour and Georgie enjoyed working with her. Being a mother to Jess meant there was little time or opportunity to socialise, so the team in the A and E department were the closest thing to friends and family—other than her brother and mother, and Jess, of course—that Georgie had.

'Eventful,' Georgie said with a smile.

'The new consultant's starting today,' Lata continued. 'Dr Hughes has called a meeting at lunchtime so we can all meet him. The place is buzzing. Apparently he's here to establish a new emergency outreach service—and he's a bit of a hunk.'

Before Georgie had a chance to quiz Lata further, or to admit that she'd already met the 'hunk', the door opened and Dr Hughes, the consultant in charge, came in with Jamie and Sarah Carruthers, the two other consultants that made up the medical team. Jamie and Sarah were married and had recently returned to the hospital after a stint in Africa. They also had a young son, who, although older than Jess, was an occasional playmate of Jess's. Georgie would take Jess with her to Sarah and Jamie's home or Sarah would bring Calum over to hers, and the two women would chat while their children played.

As usual Sarah looked jaw-droppingly gorgeous. Had it been anyone else, Georgie would have hated her on sight, but Sarah was funny and self-effacing and the two women had hit it off straight away.

'Glad to see you back,' Sarah said, dropping a kiss on Georgie's cheek. 'We missed you. How's that adorable daughter of yours?'

They caught up for a few moments before taking their seats to discuss their patients. The final member of the shift was Lizzie, the nurse in charge, who wasn't expected to join them until later as she was dealing with over-anxious parents reluctant to trust their child was over the worst.

'So tell us. What's the story behind the new consultant?' Lata asked when the report was finished.

'Everything will be revealed later, when the back shift comes in.' Dr Hughes smiled. 'In the meantime, folks, we have patients to see.'

The morning passed quickly. There was the usual mix of colds and sprains as well as broken limbs to deal with. Unusually for a Monday morning there was nothing too dramatic. Georgie grabbed a sandwich for lunch and was just making herself a coffee to wash it down when Lizzie called her into her office.

Lizzie was never one to waste time in idle chit-chat and came straight to the point.

'You've probably heard by now that we have a Dr Harris joining us for three months?'

Georgie nodded. 'I've already met him.'

Lizzie was surprised. 'You have?'

'There was a rescue on Ben Nevis at the weekend. I ended up attending. Dr Logan was part of it too. He flew in with the RAF search and rescue team. He's pretty good, from what I could see.'

'I heard about it,' Lizzie said 'There was a paragraph in the papers. But how come you were involved? I thought you'd given up working with the Lochinver Mountain Rescue?'

Georgie grinned sheepishly. 'Timing, I guess. Kirk got the callout and I just happened to be the only one he could rope in…'

'I expect a blow-by-blow when shift's over,' Lizzie said warningly.

'Okay, but there's not much to add.' Georgie tried to sound casual. 'So what *about* Dr Harris?'

'He's on loan to us from the army. All the doctors working at the front line are required to take three months off to work at civilian hospitals and he's been sent to us.'

'He'll be working in the department?' Georgie asked, her heart doing that annoying pitter-patter again.

'He specialises in acute trauma care. The army's always up to date with the latest advances in treatment. In fact, that's why he's here.'

'Oh?'

'For some time now, Glasgow NHS has been in talks with

other boards across Scotland about setting up a rapid response medical team.'

Georgie frowned. 'He mentioned it when we met, but don't we already have that?'

'I think the best thing is to let the man himself explain,' Lizzie said. 'There's a general meeting about it at the end of our shift. But seeing as you're going to be involved more closely than most, I thought we should have a chat first.'

'I am?' Georgie squeaked. This was unexpected! Her heart catapulted inside her chest.

'Yes. He's asked for you *especially*. Now I understand why. You must have impressed him.' Lizzie quirked an eyebrow, waiting for Georgie to fill her in.

Georgie's heart gave another uncomfortable kick. 'He asked for me? *Especially*?' This was getting ridiculous. She really had to stop repeating everything Lizzie said.

Before Lizzie could answer, there was a knock on the door and Logan swept in without waiting for a reply. Her heart started banging against her ribs again. Grief, was it going to do that every time she saw him?

'Here's the man himself. I'll let him explain, shall I?'

'I think that might be easier,' Georgie replied, trying not to show how flustered she felt.

Logan took the chair next to hers and stretched out long legs in front of him.

'How far have you got?' he asked Lizzie.

'Not far at all, I'm afraid. I think it's best if you explain.'

'Okay.' He leaned forward in his chair, elbows resting on his knees, his eyes locking onto hers. 'This is the way it works. We're planning to set up a team from here that will mainly, but not solely, be involved in medical emergency retrievals—or MERT, as we call it.'

'Don't we already have one of those? I mean, with the Scottish Ambulance Service?' Georgie asked.

'Up to a point. As you know, the Glasgow City Hospital will soon be the largest in the northern hemisphere, with a tertiary centre for most specialities.'

Georgie nodded. Work had started a couple of years ago to transfer paediatric services from its current stand-alone site, and the Glasgow City Hospital currently took spinal injuries from across Scotland. Add its world-class neurology wards and bring the burns and spinal units into the equation and it was easy to understand why the hospital was in the throes of a massive expansion.

'It also currently has a substantial helipad—big enough for large helicopters to land and take off, as well as being ten minutes away from Glasgow airport. It's got great advantages.'

Georgie nodded again. 'I know that the Scottish air ambulance has to land at Glasgow airport and the casualties are transferred the last few miles to us by road.'

'With the exception of having to land a few miles away from the hospital, the air ambulance can only pick up casualties where there are runways,' Lizzie interrupted. 'And that leaves the majority of Scotland's rural areas out on a limb. With the exception of the Highlands and Islands, which have their own rescue service.'

'So we use one of the other rescue services that have a helicopter for those circumstances. The navy, the RAF, the coastguard—'

Logan interrupted. 'True. Unfortunately, at the moment the air ambulance and the other rescue services currently only carry paramedics. While they can manage most emergencies very effectively, there's still a small group of people who'd survive serious injury *if*…' Logan stressed '…the helicopter was manned with a doctor and a nurse who could carry out advanced life-support procedures at the scene. Just like we currently do in the army behind the front line. We think of it as bringing the ER to the patient.'

Although it was good that the service was going to be improved, Georgie still didn't see what all this had to do with her.

Logan continued, 'London has developed a rapid medical response team, which has been running for a few years now, and as Lizzie said, the Outer Hebrides has another system, which uses doctors to go to patients who are too far from hospitals to get there quickly. But we're going to do something slightly different here. We plan to form a small team with a doctor *and* a nurse or paramedic who's trained to work to strict protocols. Unlike the current system in London, or the one in the islands, the team will only attend those emergencies where advanced life support will make the difference between life and death. We call it "grab and go" or "stay and play" in the army. We either pick up the victim and start life support immediately in the helicopter—grab and go— or if that's not possible, the doctor and paramedic do the same thing on the ground—stay and play—until the casualty is stable enough to be airlifted.' He grinned. 'I know the terminology sounds a bit frivolous, but I can assure there is nothing casual about the army service. Besides, it describes what we do excellently.' He stretched, locking his hands behind his neck.

'The Scottish Ambulance Service will continue to attend to emergencies such as women with difficult labours and other routine emergencies, but the MERT, based here, will be on call for the rest. They will go out with the RAF, navy or coastguard 'copters if required, similar to the way I did on Saturday— whenever head and spinal injuries or patients with severe breathing difficulties are suspected. Anything, in fact, where specialist resuscitation or stabilisation skills can be utilised.'

'That all sounds very interesting,' Georgie said after a silence.

'But I still don't see what it has to do with me.' Although some-where in the pit of her stomach she was beginning to have an idea.

'Easy. I want you to be on the team.'

'Me?' The question came out with another annoying squeak and she flushed.

'Yep. You. Amongst others.'

'Surely there's others better qualified. Lizzie, for example?'

Lizzie was shaking her head. 'As the department manager, I'm needed here. After me, *you're* the one with the most ex-perience and your background makes you the natural choice.'

'I need someone with a level head,' Logan continued. 'Someone who stays calm under pressure and who knows how to prioritise. Someone who is used to tricky situations and can improvise. All skills you showed in abundance on the mountain. Plus you're not scared of heights, so I assume you're not fazed by flying, or being at the end of a winch. You told me you've volunteered with the rescue medics in Fort William too. All useful, necessary experience.' He was watching her carefully.

Not scared of heights? Well, once she would have agreed. Now she wasn't so sure. 'I'm only part time,' she protested. 'That must make a difference.' Her heart was galloping. This wasn't at all what she had expected. She didn't do rescues any more. Not since Ian had died. After his death, she had decided that she couldn't risk leaving Jess without either parent. It just wouldn't be fair. And then she had moved down to Glasgow, wanting to put some distance between her and the mountains that had killed her husband. If she hadn't been in the wrong place at the wrong time, she would never have gone on Saturday either. She was finished with climbing. Finished with putting her life in danger.

But a tingle in her spine suggested otherwise. Back there on the mountain, she had been exhilarated by the rescue. She had missed being part of something where what she did made the difference between life and death. And being part of the team Logan was suggesting wouldn't mean putting herself at risk. Nerve-racking and challenging perhaps but not dangerous. She had coped with being up in the helicopter too. But Georgie knew there was another reason for the shiver of anticipation. Apart from anything else, it would mean working in close proximity with Logan. Every day. Oh, my word!

'But you're planning to be full time after the summer holidays, aren't you?' Lizzie said, bringing her back to earth. 'It'll probably take that time to get it fully operational.'

'And you won't be the only one. One of the experienced paramedics from the Scottish Ambulance Service will be trained to work opposite shifts with you. And later we'll be training Lata alongside you to cover the shifts when you aren't on duty.'

The sneaky so-and-so hadn't said a thing about it when they'd spoken earlier. Just wait until she saw her. The very least Lata could have done was warn her.

'Will you be the only doctor? Or will Sarah or Jamie be training too?'

'Eventually. But before we train other A and E specialists, I need to work with an anaesthetist to set up and agree protocols. Managing patients with compromised airways is one of the most common scenarios we'll be dealing with. Dr Fairbrother, one of the ITU consultants here, has agreed to work with me and he and I have already started to put something together. He and I will take turns in going out on calls. To begin with.'

Georgie didn't know the anaesthetist to whom Logan was referring. That was part of the problem working in a big hospital; you didn't get to meet all the staff. However, she couldn't imagine Logan selecting someone who wasn't at the top of their game to work on an initiative that was this close to his heart.

'Obviously once I return to the army, the system needs to be set up with a cohort of doctors who know and are comfortable with the protocols and procedures, and that is likely to be Sarah and Jamie, along with two or three anaesthetists and a trainee doctor.' His lips twitched. 'Dr Hughes tells me he's too long in the tooth to want to be abseiling from helicopters and learning new tricks, so I've promised him that he's off the hook. Any questions?'

It took all of Georgie's willpower not to snap 'Aye, aye, sir'. She was getting the distinct impression Major Harris was used to everyone doing exactly as he asked.

'Only one. Do I have a choice?'

Logan tipped his chair back and studied her through narrowed eyes. 'There's always a choice, Georgie,' he said softly, and she got the feeling he wasn't just talking about work.

'So what did they want you for?' Lata asked later, looking at Georgie with wide, innocent eyes. 'And are you going to do it?' she added, giving the game away. Had *everyone* known before her?

'Why didn't you tell me what they had in mind?' Georgie remonstrated.

'What? And spoil the chance of seeing that stunned look on your face? No way. Anyway, tell me, what do you think? Isn't it exciting and isn't he lovely? Pity he's not right for me or I'd be after him myself.'

Georgie laughed. Lata made no apologies for wanting to follow a traditional path. When the time was right, her parents would find her someone and she would do the right thing. Georgie never pointed out that, so far, none of her parents' choices had even been considered by Lata for longer than the introductions, and Georgie suspected that, despite her words, she secretly harboured a dream of falling instantly in love with the man her parents had chosen for her to marry.

'He's attractive,' Georgie admitted. 'If you like the action-man type. And I don't.'

'You're kidding me! What's not to like? If he's not married, I think he'd be perfect for you, Georgie.'

'He's not married,' Georgie replied without thinking.

Lata stared. 'And you know this how?'

'He told me.'

'He told you. My, that was fast work, Georgie. More and more interesting.' Lata was clearly enjoying herself. 'In which case, what's the problem?'

Why was everybody so keen these days to tell her what to do with her life? She was twenty-eight, for goodness' sake. Well able to make her own decisions. If she wanted a man in her life, she would find her own, thank you very much. And it wouldn't be Major Harris!

'Even if he were my type, I get the distinct impression he's not the kind of man who is into serious relationships. Footloose and fancy-free more like.'

Lata's smile was naughty. 'We're getting ahead of ourselves. Who said anything about a serious relationship? An *affair*, Georgie? He'd be dreamy between the sheets.'

Georgie pretended to be scandalised. 'Lata! And all this time I believed you were the demure, pure-as-snow kind!' Then she had to laugh. Lata was forever misleading people, disguising her impish humour behind a demur expression. 'And as for an affair, as you so delicately put it,' Georgie continued, shaking her head, 'uh-uh. No way. Not for me.'

Sexy as hell though he might be, Dr Logan Harris was not for her. Hadn't she already decided that she wanted nothing to do with a man like him? A man who thrived on excitement and variety? She had been there and done that. No way was she ever going to risk her heart again. Even if her libido seemed to have its own ideas.

CHAPTER FOUR

THE afternoon meeting saw the new team assembled in the meeting room. They were all there, including a petite blonde with expressive eyes who Logan introduced as Sally, a paramedic from the Scottish Ambulance Service.

While Dr Fairbrother and Logan were deep in conversation, Georgie went over to chat to Sally.

'I gather we're going to be training together,' she said, holding out her hand. 'I'm Georgie.'

'A little bit scary, don't you think?' Sally asked. 'I mean, I've attended all sorts of accidents before but this sounds even more intense. I hope I don't make a mess of it.'

Georgie smiled sympathetically. 'Me and you both.'

Logan called the meeting to order. Quickly and concisely he repeated what he had told Georgie

'We've some protocols already in place, but we'll refine them as we go along. Any questions?'

Georgie and Sally shook their heads.

'If we get called out, it's the same drill as the one you use now. You need to put on a reflective jacket and pick up the emergency medical kit. Either Dr Fairbrother—Nick—or myself will take the responsibility for the onboard medical equipment. Are we clear?'

Everyone nodded.

'In many ways it's not very different to what you do at the moment when there's a major emergency at the hospital or a callout to with the Scottish Ambulance Service…' He nodded in Sally's direction. 'The only difference is that we'll be flying out to road traffic accidents and other incidents where we'll be applying lifesaving techniques on the ground or in the air. Don't worry. There will be comprehensive training. Not just in the protocols but everyone needs to experience ditching at sea as well as being winched on and off the aircraft. Do any of you have problems with that?'

Georgie sucked in a breath. Now was the time to tell him that she wasn't sure she could do it. What if she froze again? Like she had on Saturday? Okay, she had pulled herself together and forced herself on, but what if the next time was worse? Before she could decide whether or not to say anything, Sally spoke up.

'I hate water,' she admitted. 'Can I be excused from the ditching-at-sea practice?'

'Sorry.' Logan shook his head firmly. 'It's absolutely mandatory. But why don't you see how you get on? There'll be lots of folk around to help you through the exercise. If you find…' he looked searchingly around the room '…if anyone finds that there's stuff you genuinely can't deal with, you'll be excused from the team with no hard feelings. How does that sound?'

Georgie hid a sigh of relief. There was still a get-out clause if she changed her mind.

'I'll give it a go,' Sally responded. 'I think I'll be all right, but I'm not promising anything. As long as that's understood?'

'Sure, Sally.' He nodded, his eyes sweeping the room. 'Okay, then, it's settled. We meet tomorrow morning at the training centre at HMS Gannet at Prestwick. Everybody fine for that? No one can go out on a call until they've been through the training, so the sooner we get it over the better, don't you think?'

'I think I'm supposed to be on duty tomorrow morning,' Georgie said. At the same time, Sally was muttering under her breath and shaking her head from side to side. Georgie reached out and squeezed her hand reassuringly.

Logan studied them both. 'No worries. I've arranged it all with Lizzie already. She says she'll bring in one of the other nurses to cover for you, Georgie. Ditto with you, Sally, so unless there's any other reason…?'

Sally looked as if she was about to say something, but Georgie squeezed her hand again before she spoke. 'Sally and I will see you there,' she said firmly.

Sally, Nick and Georgie were outside the training centre bang on seven o'clock the next day, but Logan was already there. Georgie and Sally had driven down together and Georgie had assured her new friend that they'd make it through the morning—together—no matter what it took.

Logan seemed remarkably upbeat and fresh for seven a.m. Then again, he'd probably run ten miles this morning, Georgie thought resentfully. It was all right for him. He had spent years training in all sorts of scenarios and conditions.

Nick appeared relaxed as well. No doubt some macho thing kept him from showing his apprehension. Either that or he genuinely wasn't worried. And neither was she, Georgie realised. In some ways she was even looking forward to the challenge. Water had never bothered her. But, then, neither had heights— until recently.

Sally, on the other hand, seemed utterly miserable. Georgie realised it would take courage for her to make it through the challenge but, despite Sally's anxiety, Georgie could tell by the set of her mouth that the paramedic was determined to complete the task.

'We strap you into your seat,' Logan was saying.

He looks sexy as hell in his body-hugging wetsuit, Georgie thought, before telling herself crossly that she needed to concentrate on the task in hand.

'Then we lower the mock-up helicopter into the water and as soon as it's submerged, we invert the craft. At that point you unbuckle your belt and make your way to the surface. You may find that at first you're disoriented. Try not to panic. Feel your way to the door and push yourself out. Remember, if anyone looks as if they're in trouble, I and the other divers will be standing by to help you to the surface.'

'What happens if I can't unbuckle my belt?' Sally asked. Although she looked pale, her voice was steady.

'As I said, if you find at any stage you can't do something, someone will help you out.' Logan grinned. 'I really don't want to lose anyone. Our job is to save lives, not kill people. We'll have a practice run where I'll be in the seat next to you, just in case, and then you'll do it on your own—for real.'

'Why can't we do it two at a time?' Sally asked

'Because I don't want any of you thinking about helping your partner instead of getting yourselves out.' He looked at Nick. 'There's no room for chivalry.'

Georgie was about to protest when Logan winked at her and Sally. 'And that goes for everyone.'

The experience wasn't as bad as Georgie expected. Then again, she was used to staying calm under pressure, even if this was a completely different kind of pressure than any of them were used to. Knowing that Logan and the divers were standing by ready to help if anybody got into trouble helped. Of course, if it ever happened in real life, it would be different, much more scary, but Georgie made up her mind that she wouldn't even think of it being a possibility.

Even Sally managed, although it took her a couple of extra attempts. Logan kept reassuring her that she was doing fine and telling her that he was sure she'd do it, until finally and triumphantly she did.

Logan was pleased. 'Okay, everyone passed. That's the first test. The next one involves some abseiling and getting used to being winched from the aircraft, but I don't anticipate any difficulties. I'm hoping to schedule it for a few weekends' time.' He named a date. 'So keep it free, please.'

Georgie felt a shiver of anxiety. Little did Logan know it was the part of the training she was dreading the most. There was no point in worrying about it now. She would face that when the time came. At least if she froze again, she wouldn't be putting anyone else's life in danger.

Thankfully there were showers and everyone retreated to freshen up and change back into their clothes.

Georgie left Sally to finish reapplying her make-up, and went back out into the corridor. Logan was leaning against the wall, talking into his phone. The way he was grinning made Georgie certain it was some woman he was talking to. Once again she felt an unwelcome stab of disappointment.

'Until tonight. I'll be looking forward to it,' Logan said, before flipping his phone shut. So she was right. He had been making a date. What else had she expected? Logan wasn't the kind of man not to have someone in tow.

'Hey. All ready? How did you find it?'

'Not as scary as I thought,' Georgie admitted. 'Although I hope with all my heart I never have to do it for real.'

'Me too.' He smiled. 'Scottish waters aren't known for their warmth.'

Without warning, he reached across and touched her cheek gently. 'You're bruised.'

His touch sent tiny shocks coursing through her and before she could stop herself she took a step back, her hand going to the place where the touch of his fingers burned her skin.

'Oh, that.' She tried a laugh, but somehow it came out all strangled. 'I bumped myself on the door of the helicopter when I was trying to find the way out. It's nothing.'

There was an uncomfortable silence for a moment as their eyes locked before Sally, her make-up in place, came rushing out of the bathroom.

'That's me. All ready to go.'

She looked at Georgie and Logan, clearly sensing something.

Georgie unglued her feet from the floor and with one last weak smile at Logan grabbed Sally's arm and hustled her out of the door and away from the appraising look in Logan's eyes.

A few days later, Logan and Georgie were in the staffroom with Jamie and Sarah, enjoying a break after the morning rush. Georgie was surprised how quickly and easily Logan had fitted into the department. Jamie, in particular, seemed to enjoy having someone around to talk football and rugby with. He was always pretending to complain that Sarah had no interest in either sport.

Not for the first time, Georgie found herself envious of Jamie and Sarah. They were so obviously in love, so deeply in tune with one another, it made her miss being part of a couple. Sarah, however, had admitted to Georgie that her romance with Jamie hadn't always run smoothly and that she had even hidden Calum's birth from him. Nevertheless, whatever problems they had faced in the past, it was evident that little troubled them now.

Lizzie popped her head round the door, interrupting Georgie's musing.

'Looks like you have your first shout.' She wrinkled her brow. 'Shout's the right word, isn't it?' She rushed on without waiting for a reply. 'The Royal Navy's been called out from Prestwick. Trouble off the coast of Oban. Apparently a fisherman is in trouble. He's been stung by a bee and is having difficulty breathing. The navy is asking for a medical team to go on board. What shall I tell them?'

'It sounds right up our street. Tell them to pick us up. When is their ETA?' Logan replied, already on his feet.

'Not sure,' Lizzie said. 'I needed to check you were happy to attend. I'll get back to you as soon as I know.'

Logan turned to Georgie. 'Are you up for this?'

Before she had time to think, Georgie was on her feet. 'Of course.' Adrenaline shot through her veins. She was damned if she was going to let her fear stop her from even trying. One way or another, she would cope.

'Okay. Grab a fluorescent jacket. The helicopter will have a life vest and a helmet.'

Lizzie popped her head back through the door. 'They'll be landing on the helipad in three minutes.' She shoved two brightly coloured jackets at Georgie. 'I fished these out of our major incident cupboard for you.' She grinned. 'Good luck.'

Quickly Georgie and Logan shrugged themselves into the jackets. Logan's had 'Doctor' emblazoned on the back of his while she had 'Nurse'. It made it easier for everyone involved in the rescue to know who was who.

Logan was running out the door towards the helipad, leaving Georgie to do her best to keep up. As soon as they were outside the hospital building they could hear the powerful beating of the large helicopter's rotor blades.

'Keep your head down and follow me.' Logan shouted to make himself heard above the deafening beat of the blades. He reached behind him and, grabbing her hand, pulled her towards the navy aircraft. It was just as well he had a firm grip on her, Georgie thought. The downdraught felt as if it could pick her up off her feet and blow her away.

Hands reached out to pull them inside and the helicopter lifted off, banking sharply. One of the men inside held out a helmet and life vest for each of them. He also passed Logan a microphone to attach to his headgear. All Georgie was given was a pair of earphones to reduce some of the noise.

Logan was speaking into the mike, but Georgie couldn't hear a word he was saying. After a moment he leaned towards her, pushing aside one of the earphones so he could shout in her ear.

'The crew are in touch with the fishing vessel. The patient is still breathing, but only just. It's clearly anaphylactic shock. Unfortunately they don't have adrenaline on board the boat. Our job is simple. All we have to do is keep him alive until we get him to hospital in Oban. The local team will take over from there.'

Georgie simply nodded. She was trying not to think about being hundreds of feet above the ground. Instead, she forced herself to look around the helicopter. It was much bigger inside than she had imagined and as long as she couldn't see outside she could almost pretend she was on the ground. Almost—but not quite.

Ten minutes later they were hovering over the sea and the winchman opened the door. A rush of nausea hit Georgie as she saw the sea a few hundred feet below coming into view. Don't think about it, she warned herself. Just concentrate on what you have to do.

The winchman was gesticulating somewhere ahead, but Georgie couldn't see the boat. But he must have, as he started preparing to let himself out over the side.

'The boat has to keep moving so not to be caught in the he-

licopter's downdraft,' Logan yelled in her ear again. 'The helicopter will match its speed then let the winchman down to
have a look-see. He'll administer adrenaline. If needed, he'll
winch me down so I can assess the casualty on board. But he
won't do that unless he thinks it's necessary. We'll just be
wasting valuable time otherwise.'

Logan's eyes were dancing. He loves this, Georgie thought.
He loves the whole excitement and danger of it. She suspected
if he had his way, he'd be down that rope before anyone could
stop him. But he was too much the professional to let his own
desires get in the way of good practice. What was it about certain men that they seemed to thrive in danger? With a sinking
heart she recognised that she and Ian had shared the same love
of danger. Maybe that was why she was attracted to Logan?
Aghast, she dipped her head dreading the thought that he might
be able to read her mind.

They were closer now and the winchman had disappeared
over the side. Unable to bring herself to join Logan at the door,
where he was peering after him, Georgie busied herself
checking the oxygen and the portable monitor. Everything was
working perfectly.

Then Logan was pulling the winchman and the casualty
on board. Immediately Georgie could tell the patient was in
a bad way. He was barely conscious, and his lips were tinged
with blue. Either he was hypothermic or suffering from a
lack of oxygen or both. Years of training took over as she
fitted the oxygen mask over the injured man's mouth and
helped the crewman wrap him in blankets. While they were
doing that, Logan was checking his vital signs and adminis-
tering adrenaline.

'Pulse 126, BP 78 over 42, O2 sat 78 per cent—he's certainly shocked,' Logan shouted to them.

'And short of oxygen,' Georgie added, taking his oxygen mask off briefly. 'His air passages and tongue are swollen from the sting restricting his airway.'

'It's very difficult in the helicopter to hear anything—the stethoscope is a waste of time. We'd better assume he's wheezy, causing the low oxygen saturation.' Logan spoke his thoughts out loud.

'Okay, I'll get the nebuliser out of the bag. How long till we get to Oban?'

Georgie could hear bits of Logan's conversation with the pilot as she drew up the nebuliser solution. It had been ten minutes since the adrenaline had been given and his oxygen sats had risen to 82 per cent. His condition was starting to improve.

'He's holding up,' she shouted, as Logan came alongside to help her.

'It's only four minutes before we land and the ground team should be on standby.' Logan gave her a wide smile. 'Think you're going to enjoy being part of the team?'

She knew she didn't have to say anything. Despite her vertigo, Georgie had loved every minute of it and she knew it was written all over her face.

By the time the helicopter dropped them back at the hospital, Georgie's shift was over. She could hardly believe how quickly the hours had flown. As she was gathering her belongings together, ready to leave, Logan appeared.

'You did very well.'

'Thank you,' Georgie replied.

'Have dinner with me,' he said abruptly.

It wasn't really a question and the suddenness took her breath away. Flustered, she could only open and close her mouth like an idiot.

'I…I have to see my daughter,' she managed through a throat as dry as dust.

'After she's in bed, then. She must have a bedtime, and didn't you say your mother was staying with you? Couldn't she stay with Jess?'

'Yes. But she's already had Jess all day. I couldn't ask her to babysit tonight too.' That wasn't the real reason she was prevaricating and they both knew it. Once Jess was in bed, that was usually her for the night. She wouldn't be any bother. Why couldn't she just be honest? She took a deep breath and her courage in both hands.

'I don't know if I'm ready to date again.'

She flushed as she realised what she'd said. What if she was jumping the gun and this wasn't a date at all? Maybe he was only asking her as a colleague he'd be working closely with? Her and her big mouth.

'I mean *if* it is a date…' Her flush deepened as he grinned widely.

'That's kind of what I had in mind.' His eyes dropped to the ring finger of her left hand. 'Perhaps you're right,' he said softly. 'But, Georgie, I only had dinner in mind. That's all.'

Her heart was thudding uncomfortably in her chest. What should she do? There was no doubt she found him attractive, almost painfully so. And it wasn't only a physical attraction either; there was a connection between her and this man. A connection that went far beyond physical attraction. She could fall for him. Fall for him in a big way. And she just couldn't take that chance. It wasn't just his career. A career that took him all over the world, never settling in one place. Never allowing him to put down roots. That was one thing. No way did she want to lead that kind of life again, and no way did she want it for her daughter either.

No, it was more. Hadn't she repeatedly told herself that she would never want to be with a man who put his life in danger almost every day of his life? Logan would be gone in three months. Far better that she keep her distance. Even if every nerve cell in her body was refusing to listen to her brain.

On the other hand, it *was* just dinner. What was the harm in that? Two colleagues sharing a meal.

Confused by the conflicting emotions whizzing around her brain, she shook her head. 'I don't know. I'll have to think about it.'

Logan took a step back, surprise written all over his face. Georgie guessed that he wasn't used to being turned down.

'Of course,' he said smoothly. 'I understand. Maybe another time?'

'Sure,' Georgie mumbled. 'Sorry, I've got to run.' And before he could say anything else, she took off as if the devil himself were behind her.

Bemused, Logan watched her retreating back. It was the first time he could remember that he'd been turned down when he'd asked a woman out. He whistled under his breath. He hadn't got it wrong, he was sure of it. She found him attractive, he could tell. So, what was it then—could his instinct be wrong? He shook his head. No. It wasn't. She was attracted to him. He could see it in the way she pinked up when he looked at her, in the way she dropped her eyes under his gaze. He knew enough about women to know he hadn't misread the situation. But Georgie was different from any other woman he had been with, he also knew that. Could it be that she was still in love with her dead husband? She was still wearing her wedding ring, a sure sign that she still thought of herself as married. In which case it was unfair of him to pursue her. Especially when he had no intention of getting too involved. On the other hand, was it wrong to want to bring a smile to that mouth? To see her laugh again? He ignored the inner voice that was telling him that the argument going on inside his head was one that suited him. All he knew for sure was that he wasn't ready yet to give up on Georgie McArthur. He would just have to try a different approach.

His thoughts turned to his mother. For some reason, ever since he had met Georgie he had kept thinking of the woman who had given birth to him. Perhaps it was because in Georgie he had seen how a mother could be—no, *should* be—with a child. Maybe his mother had had no choice when she'd given him up; maybe even loved him the way Georgie loved Jess? Perhaps it was time he tried to get in touch with her and give her a chance to tell her side of the story. At the very least he would find out whether she was still alive, whether she was okay. Whatever she had done in the past, surely he owed it to himself—and to her—to find out the truth. Even if she rejected him all over again, he was a grown man now. What harm could it possibly do?

Georgie finished putting Jess to bed and then ran herself a hot bath. Her mother was downstairs, watching her favourite gardening programme on TV, and would be happily engrossed for the next hour.

Logan asking her out had taken her by surprise. Should she have taken a chance and said yes? As he'd said, it was just dinner—not a lifetime commitment. For the last few years she had concentrated on being a mother, caring for her daughter. Between that and work there'd been no time for anything else. But Georgie knew that for her at least it wasn't just a meal with some casual acquaintance, and that was the problem. Logan made her heart race—that grin of his, the twinkle in his eyes, the way he made her conscious of her femininity again. She knew she could fall for Logan Harris. Fall in a big way. And there was no way he was the kind of man she should let herself become involved with. No. It was safer to keep her distance. He wouldn't be around for ever. And if she wasn't very careful he would take her heart with him.

CHAPTER FIVE

THE next couple of weeks passed without a callout. At least, not for her. Sally had gone out with Logan to a walker with a suspected stroke when Georgie had been off duty. Happily the clot-busting drugs they had administered at the scene had worked and the man was on his way to a full recovery.

The new service was creating a buzz within the hospital and Georgie was proud to be part of it.

Over the last couple of weeks there had been regular meetings to go over protocols and when they weren't doing that, Logan was spending every free moment with the other rescue services, finalising arrangements. Logan quizzed her and Sally constantly until he was sure that they were both comfortable with the protocols and knew exactly what to do for each type of incident.

'We can't have protocols for everything,' Logan admitted. 'There are too many variants to each scenario, but the basic principles are the same: maintain an airway and contain bleeding until arrival at hospital. In its simplest form, we keep the casualty alive until the A and E team takes over.'

He hadn't asked her out again and Georgie didn't know whether she was relieved or disappointed. All she knew was that every time she saw him, her heart beat faster. Even the sight of him from a distance caused a nervous flutter in her stomach.

'Remember, folks, this Saturday is the team-building day. I'm planning on taking my car so we can all go together.'

'Remind me what it involves,' Sally said anxiously.

'The day falls into two parts. In the morning we go over the protocols Nick and I have drawn up. Yes, yet again.' He smiled as everyone groaned. 'After lunch we'll move on to the team-building part of the day. It involves some abseiling, some high ropes and starts with off-road driving. Nothing too complicated.'

'Nothing too complicated for you and Georgie perhaps. You do that sort of thing all the time. Georgie is a climber,' Sally muttered. 'I have never even climbed higher than my own height. The water thing…' She shuddered. 'That was bad enough.'

At one time, Sally would have been right; it wouldn't have fazed Georgie in the slightest. But that was before…before she had begun to lose her nerve. Her stomach clenched with anxiety. What if she couldn't perform? What if she couldn't cope? She'd be put off the team and now that was the last thing she wanted. She gritted her teeth. She was damned if she would give up before they'd even started and let her fear get the better of her. After all, she'd managed to put it behind her when they'd taken Jack off the mountain, hadn't she? And she'd coped in the helicopter too. Just as long as she wasn't looking down at the ground from a height.

'We'll take good care of you, Sally.' Logan grinned. 'Don't worry, it'll be a piece of cake. Now, what about transport?'

'Sally and I are on the same side of the city,' Nick said. 'Why don't I pick her up in the morning and you take Georgie? That will save time.'

'Fine with me.' Brown eyes swept the room, before they found hers. 'Georgie?'

Georgie nodded. 'What time?'

'We need to be there around 0900 hours. It'll take a couple of hours. So say 0700?'

Georgie hid a smile. Years with the army had left its mark on Logan. Just in time she stopped herself from saluting.

'Suits me,' she said instead.

After a sleepless night tossing and turning, Georgie was ready and waiting when on the dot of seven Logan's two-seater pulled up outside. She watched as he swung his legs out of the car and marched up to her door. He was wearing a T-shirt that clung to his chest, outlining every honed muscle clearly. Faded blue jeans emphasised the contours of his thighs in the most discon-certing manner. Georgie sucked in a breath as heat pooled in her abdomen.

Before he could ring the bell, she had opened the door. Jess was at the breakfast table, finishing her cereal under the watchful eyes of her grandmother. Georgie kissed her goodbye.

'I'll be back later tonight, sweetheart. Granny will look after you.'

Jess's eyes lit up when she saw Logan. Before anyone could stop her she was out of her chair and had rushed across the room to fling herself into Logan's arms.

'Uncle Logan,' she yelped. Logan had no option but to lift the little girl. Bemused brown eyes met Georgie's.

'Hello, sweetie. It's good to see you too.' It was the first time Georgie had seen him looking flustered. Gently he set Jess back down on the floor. 'How are you, Mrs Morrison?' he asked Georgie's mother politely. If Georgie didn't know better she would have sworn her mother blushed. Damn the man. Did he have this effect on every woman he met?

'Please call me Mary,' her mother replied. 'I've organised a flask of coffee and some home-made biscuits.' Mary smiled coquettishly and Georgie wanted to kick her. 'In case you get hungry.'

Logan's eyes lit up. 'Thank you, ma'am. It's been a while since breakfast.' *A while since breakfast? It was only seven!*

Logan must have noticed her astonishment. 'Remember I get up at six most mornings and I almost always go for a run. Army habit, I'm afraid. So by this time I'm usually starving again.'

Silently, Georgie unwrapped a piece of shortbread and handed it to him. He devoured it in a couple of bites. 'Hey, great baking.'

Mary blushed again and Georgie knew that Logan had won her mother over. 'I'll just pop in some of my cheese scones, in that case.'

As Georgie's mother turned away, Logan grinned at Georgie. 'Are you ready?' Georgie's heart thumped. This wasn't good. Wasn't good at all.

'We need to get going, Mum.' She practically snatched the scones from her mother's hands. Any longer and Mary would be adopting Logan, inviting him for dinner, offering him the spare room. She had seen the look in her mother's eyes and knew exactly what she was thinking. For the last year or so she'd been pushing Georgie to start dating again. But whatever plan she was hatching would have to be shelved. Logan Harris was *not* the man for her.

Logan drove the way he seemed to do everything—as fast as possible. Noticing that Georgie was gripping the edge of her seat, he grinned.

'Hey, relax,' he said, 'before you dig holes in my car seat with your nails.'

'We *have* got two hours to get there,' she admonished through gritted teeth. 'And I have a child I don't want to see orphaned.' As soon as the words were out she could have bitten her tongue.

The smile left his face and he slowed the car to a more sedate pace.

'Sorry.'

They drove on. The sun was rising in the sky, clearing the final traces of mist from the distant hills. It would be warm later on, Georgie knew. They sat in silence as they left the city behind them.

'What happened to Jess's dad?' Logan said suddenly.

Before she could help herself, Georgie covered her left hand with her right. She still wasn't ready to talk about Ian. At least, not to Logan.

He must have seen the stricken look on her face. 'Sorry. Forget I asked. It's none of my business.'

For a moment there was a strained silence.

'What about you? Have you ever wanted to get married?' she asked. Once again, the words were out before she could stop herself. There was only one interpretation he could put on her question. Why, oh, why had she asked? Why did she feel so nervous in his company and feel driven to say the first thing that popped into her head?

'Nope. Not the marrying kind. As far as I can tell, marriage is overrated. I guess the army is as much of a wife as I need. It would take a special woman to put up with being an army wife, I guess. Someone who doesn't mind moving all the time.'

'How can you bear it?' Georgie asked. 'Never being able to put down roots. Always travelling. My dad was in the army, and I hated that we were always on the move. Mum always seemed so lonely, although she denied it. Despite what she always said about having Kirk and I for company, we couldn't have been enough for her. And what about the constant danger? Why do some men seem to thrive on putting their lives at risk?' She couldn't help the note of bitterness that crept into her voice. Ian had been like that.

And looked what had happened. It seemed so unfair that the first man she found attractive since Ian shared that need.

Logan looked at her curiously. 'I can't imagine doing anything else,' he said quietly. 'The army helped me turn my life around and has given me opportunities I would never have had otherwise. As for the danger...' He shrugged and his hand strayed briefly to the scar below his eye. 'I'm a doctor. It's my job to go where I'm needed. The danger I face is nothing compared to those who are actually fighting.' His jaw clenched and Georgie wondered what had happened to bring that bleak look to his eyes.

'What opportunities?'

'Let's just say I wasn't the most well-behaved teenager. The army helped channel what could have been destructive energy into something that gave me direction when I needed it most.'

'Like?' Georgie persisted.

'Like sport. I was always good at school but I didn't take studying seriously. When I joined the army cadets when I was thirteen, I realised I was really good at lots of different sports. After that I started doing the military pentathlon every year. It keeps me focused.' He looked thoughtful. 'Once I stopped mucking around, I realised I was also clever enough to go to university. The army put me through med school.'

She noticed he still didn't talk about who had brought him up. Although she was intensely curious, for once she was going to keep her mouth shut. Logan would tell her when and if he was ready. 'What's a pentathlon?' she asked. 'I know I've heard the term somewhere but I can't think now what it is.'

He laughed. A deep, rich sound. 'A combination of shooting, fencing, horse riding, swimming and cross-country. It's supposed to simulate a nineteenth-century cavalryman behind enemy lines. You know, where he could grab a horse, fight his way out of trouble with a gun or his sword, before hightailing it across water or open fields.'

Georgie whistled. 'And you do all of those things? Competitively? Cripes, no wonder…' She bit her lip. She'd been just about to say no wonder he had a body like he did but, thank the lord, she had stopped herself in time. Unfortunately she wasn't able to stop the blush stealing up to her face.

'Yep. It still keeps me out of trouble.' But the look he slid her way told her he was thinking of a different kind of trouble. One that involved a totally different type of sport.

'And let me guess—you jump out of planes too.'

''Fraid so. And fly 'em.'

Definitely not the man for her, then. The last thing she needed was to fall for another adrenaline junkie. She'd do well to remember that. Why, then, did her heart twist with disappointment?

By the time they arrived, Sally and Nick were already there, sipping coffee. The sun had burnt off the last remaining clouds and the day was going to be hot and dry. In the distance, Georgie could see the top of a mountain she had climbed and felt a pang. Sarah, who climbed regularly with Jamie, was always asking her to go with them, but Georgie always found some excuse, offering to babysit Calum for them instead. She was only now beginning to realise how much of her life she had shut away when Ian had died. But, she reminded herself, she had Jess. And her daughter was everything that mattered.

'I've organised some gear for all of us,' Logan explained. 'We'll get into it later. No point right now. After lunch will be soon enough.'

Georgie's heart began to race as she contemplated the afternoon. Would she cope? Apart from not being on the team, she hated the thought of failing in Logan's eyes. Damn it! She hated the thought of failing in her own eyes.

The afternoon came all too soon. The morning was easy; the protocols straightforward. Nothing that Georgie couldn't cope with, although she knew being out there at the scene of the accident would be very different. No amount of training could prepare them for all the circumstances they might face. However, Logan's matter-of-fact tone when he described situations he'd been in made her realise that keeping a steady head was the most important thing. And she was good at that. She had to be to work in A and E.

After lunch they gathered outside.

'We're going to start with off-road driving,' Logan said.

'What's that got to do with medical rescue?' Sally asked. 'We're not expected to do any driving as part of our role, are we? Next you'll be telling us we have to learn how to fly a helicopter.'

Logan grinned again. 'No. You can relax. Piloting lessons most definitely not required. Much of today is about testing skills you'll need when out on a rescue. Like being lowered from a helicopter or being winched aboard. Before we go on to that, I need to see how you cope with heights, how you react under duress, whether you can trust each other enough to perform even when you're not sure that what you're being asked to do is right. At a scene we might have multiple casualties to deal with. It's Nick's job, or mine, to prioritise. Sometimes you might not agree with our decisions, but it's essential you do what we ask.'

'But the off-road driving?' Georgie persisted. 'I still don't get it. I see the point of the other activities, but driving a four by four...?'

'Ah. But this is driving with a difference. We're all going to take it in turns at being blindfolded at the wheel. The driver will then have to trust their co-driver to give them instructions.'

'You've got to be kidding,' Sally spluttered. 'I have enough of a back-seat driver with my father! He's always telling me I drive too fast or too slow or something!'

Everyone laughed.

'I don't know,' Nick said slowly.' Sounds like fun. I've always wanted to do a bit of off-road driving. Not so sure about the blindfold, though.'

Nick rarely said much, seeming content to only chip in when his input was needed. He was almost the opposite of Logan—quiet when Logan was bursting with barely suppressed energy. But he had a calm assurance about him that Georgie found re-assuring. In many ways, Logan had done a good job bringing his fledgling team together. Too many similar personalities could have caused problems and disagreements.

'It's more about trust than driving,' Logan continued. 'We all get a practice run without the blindfold then we take it in turns to be the driver and co-driver. I'll partner Sally while Georgie partners Nick, then Sally goes with Nick while I go with Georgie and so on. Any questions?'

Everyone shook their heads. Logan and Sally went off to the vehicle with an instructor while Georgie and Nick went to the other.

In the end it turned out to be more fun than scary. Driving up and down steep slopes took a bit of getting used to, but was manageable. After the practice run, they swapped, Logan joining Georgie, and Nick accompanying Sally.

Logan took his turn with the blindfold first while Georgie told him where to go. When she said right, he turned without hesitation. Ditto when she said left or down or faster or slower. Whatever she asked, he did.

Then it was her turn.

He placed the blindfold over her eyes. 'Trust me,' he said in her ear. His breath, warm against her neck, gave her goose bumps. Oh, my word, could he just not do that? How did he expect her to concentrate?

'Just do what I ask, and you'll be fine,' he continued.

Georgie knew about trust. Out on rescues, the team had to trust each other without question. There were often moments when all that stood between you and a fall was the person holding the lead rope. If you doubted them, you would never climb. Trust was what made the team work and up until Ian's death they had always managed to pull each other through. And Ian's death had nothing to do with the rest of the team, although she suspected that Kirk blamed himself. They all knew the risks. Or at least she had thought they had. Sure, she had always known that the mountain could kill, but Ian was the first person close to her who had died on the mountains, and, apart from her father, he'd been one of the best climbers she'd ever known.

Her mind raced back to that day. It had been winter and a layer of snow had covered the mountains. Despite being warned against it, a group of climbers had gone up the mountain. When they'd failed to return by nightfall, the mountain rescue team had been alerted. Georgie, with a baby to look after, hadn't been asked to attend the rescue, but as always Ian had insisted on going. Kirk had been there too, but even his skill had been unable to prevent the tragedy that had followed. Although she knew it was illogical, in her darkest moments Georgie couldn't stop the flood of anger when she thought about Ian's senseless death. Why couldn't he have stayed at home for once? Why did he always have to be the first person to volunteer?

'All right, Georgie?' Logan's voice brought her out of her reverie. She nodded and started to drive. At first she was so tentative the car barely moved. But soon, under Logan's soft confident instructions, she relaxed and found herself doing what he asked without any hesitation. Instinctively she knew he would never put her in danger.

When they stopped and she was able to pull off her blindfold, she grinned with relief. Logan smiled back, his toffee-coloured eyes approving.

'Hey, not bad for a girl.'

When she took a playful swipe at him, he caught her hand and held it. She felt the pad of his thumb trace the inside most sensitive part of her wrist, and she had to bite down hard to stop the groan that bubbled to her lips. Heat soared through her veins, setting her nerve endings alight. Aghast, she pulled her hand away. What was she thinking? Only minutes before she had been remembering her dead husband yet here she was responding to a man, and not just any man either. The man who was in too many fundamental ways like her husband. If Ian's death had taught her nothing else, it had taught her that loving was risky. Far too risky.

Logan looked surprised when she pulled her hand away and she prayed she wasn't blushing again.

They swapped round and it was her turn with Nick. By this time she had got the hang of it. Nick was a steady, relaxed guide around the course and seemed to have no problem following her directions when it was his turn to be blindfolded. The last round involved her and Sally. That didn't go quite as well. Sally kept trying to steal glances at the road from under the blindfold. When it was Georgie's turn to be blindfolded, Sally somehow—Georgie wasn't quite sure how—managed to direct her into a ditch. After seeing where they were, they dissolved in a fit of giggles.

'C'mon, Georgie, let's get out of here before they see us,' Sally said when they had stopped laughing. 'Never mind the blindfold, do whatever it takes. The last thing I want is our two male colleagues feeling that they have to rescue us and muttering under their breath about female drivers.'

'Me neither.' Georgie agreed wholeheartedly. 'I suspect they'd never let us forget it.'

It took a fair bit of effort and testing of their new-found skills, but soon they had the vehicle pointing in the right direction once more. Georgie replaced her blindfold before they were spotted and managed to bring the four by four to a controlled stop at just the right place. Unsurprisingly, Nick and Logan were there before them. If they were anything like the men she knew, and she strongly suspected they were, they had probably competed with each other all the way round. However, if there was friendly rivalry between the two men, there was no evidence of it in their relaxed manner with one another.

'Okay. Now for the abseiling. I know you will have done this before, Georgie, so I suspect it'll be a piece of cake for you. As far as I know, neither Nick nor Sally have, though.'

Georgie's heart hammered against her ribs. This was the moment she'd been dreading. But she knew she couldn't avoid it. Either she would freeze, in which case she was off the team, or she wouldn't. Either way her role in the team would be decided.

As they put on their harnesses, Georgie's heart continued to race. If Logan noticed she was quiet he gave no hint, being too engrossed in making sure Sally and Nick's harnesses were properly secured. When he had finished with them he crossed over to her.

'I know you're used to doing this yourself, but I need to check, okay?'

Georgie nodded, her mouth too dry to speak. As Logan fiddled around with the straps, his fingers brushing against her body, her knees felt as if they wouldn't support her for much

longer. But whether that was from his touch or fear of the next
half an hour or so, Georgie couldn't tell.

'Okay. Who wants to go first?'

Georgie followed his eyes upwards. First there was a high
pole with steel pins to climb. From there two lines of steel were
strung across the gap, which led to a small platform. Each par-
ticipant would have to balance on the lower steel wire while
using the higher one to balance. Once on the platform there was
a higher level to climb up to. From there, they would abseil
down a wall. The last bit would probably be fine, but would she
cope with her vertigo at the point where she had to cross the
gap? There was only one way to find out.

'I'll go,' Georgie volunteered, relieved to find her voice
steady. If she couldn't do it, now was the time to find out.
Much better to find out now instead of when in an aircraft and
about to be winched down to some casualty. Whatever her
terror of being exposed like this, her horror of letting a casualty
down was far worse.

She started climbing the pole, her blood thumping in her
ears. Don't look down, she told herself. It was the same thing
she had told countless people when she had been taking them
off mountains. Just keep looking up, or straight ahead.

She was shaking when she reached the first platform. She
forced herself not to look down. Instead, she measured the
distance to the next platform with a practised eye. Gingerly she
stepped out on the wire, gasping as it swayed with her weight.

Before she could help herself she glanced down. A wave of
vertigo washed over her, nauseating her. She swallowed hard.
*Pretend you are on the ground, following a line. Think of some-
thing else and keep moving.* Unfortunately the only image
strong enough to divert her attention away from the ground was
six feet three with toffee-coloured eyes and a body that took

her breath away. So be it. As she moved across the wire, she let her mind dwell on narrow hips and long muscular legs. What would it be like to have those arms wrapped around her, holding her tight against his chest, the muscles rippling under her cheek? She almost groaned aloud and just stopped herself from closing her eyes. Delicious. That's how it would feel.

Then she was on the second platform. It swayed slightly in the wind. But her fear was ebbing away. In its place was the old thrill of pushing her body, testing its limits, making it obey her commands no matter how impossible those demands seemed at the time. She stretched her arms to the sky, revelling in the rush of air against her skin. It felt good. She had beaten one fear. Could she beat another? Wasn't it time she stopped hiding from all that life had to offer?

Exhilarated, she abseiled down to the bottom where Logan was waiting.

'Well done,' he called to her. But something in his voice made her wonder whether he had noticed her hesitation at the beginning. If he had, would he be beginning to doubt her? Before she could say anything, Nick slid down next to her. He must have followed immediately. That just left Sally, who was nervously waiting her turn. And Logan.

Sally was looking understandably nervous.

'I'll go in front of you and Georgie or Nick will go behind you,' Logan said reassuringly. 'It's okay to be scared, but you'll cope just fine.'

With a look at Georgie, which suggested Sally held her accountable for the predicament she found herself in, Sally followed Logan hesitatingly up the pole.

'Shall I?' Nick asked with a tip of his head. He didn't wait for a reply but immediately followed Sally. Georgie could hear his voice urging Sally on whenever she hesitated, which was surprisingly little. Sally hesitated only once before making her way across the rope to the platform and abseiling down the wall. It seemed that they had all underestimated her grit once again. Georgie felt like cheering, knowing how much it meant to Sally that the women in the team were seen to be on par with the men.

The mood was buoyant as they stripped off their overalls.

'Who fancies stopping off for a celebratory meal on the way home?' Logan asked. 'I think we deserve it.'

Sally's face fell. 'Sorry. I promised I'd be home for dinner. My parents are having guests and I told them I'd join them.' She grimaced and Georgie had the uneasy feeling that, whoever these guests were, Sally wasn't looking forward to their company.

'I'll drop you off, then,' Nick said cheerfully. 'We can all get together for dinner another time.'

'What about you, Georgie?' Logan asked.

She could be mistaken but she thought her reply really mattered to him. Could he be lonely? Was he really as self-sufficient as he liked to make out? After all, he was probably used to being surrounded by people all the time. She had the impression, although she could be completely wrong, that men in the forces spent all their time together. However, Logan didn't strike her as someone who needed to be with other people. Quite the opposite, in fact. There was a confidence about him that said he was used to relying on himself. His invite was what it was. One colleague seeking out the companionship of another.

But she had been away from Jess for the whole day and she saw little enough of her daughter.

'I'm sorry,' she said, genuinely regretful. 'Another time perhaps? I've a little girl waiting for me at home.' Then impulsively, before she could help herself, she added, 'But why not join us for dinner tomorrow? It's Mum's birthday and I've booked us a table at Rogano's as a treat. I'm sure they'll make space for one more and Jess would love to see you again.'

A strange look crossed Logan's face.

'I don't want to intrude on a family celebration,' he said mildly. 'Why don't we make it another time when we're all free?'

Georgie cringed inwardly, feeling the heat rise in her cheeks. Did he think she was making a move on him? Trying him out as a father fit for her daughter? How absolutely mortifying.

They said their goodbyes and soon Georgie and Logan were racing back to Glasgow. This time the silence was uncomfortably strained.

Georgie was relieved when the sound of a mobile ringing broke the silence.

'Would you like me to answer for you?' she asked. Logan nodded and Georgie pressed button to accept the call.

'Darling, where have you been all day?' The voice was low, throaty and unmistakably feminine.

'Sorry. This is one of Logan's colleagues. He's driving and can't take the call right now. Shall I ask him to call you back?'

'If you could, that would be lovely,' the voice answered.

'Who shall I say…?'

A husky laugh travelled down the line. 'Logan will know who it is. Tell him I'll be waiting for his call.' And with that she disconnected.

Georgie stared at the phone before folding it closed. Whoever the woman was, she knew Logan intimately. She felt a rush of disappointment.

'Er…she didn't say who it was—but you're to call her.'

Logan flicked her a glance. 'Camilla.'

Why should she be surprised? A man like Logan was bound to be involved with someone. So she had read more into his invitation than he had intended. Then again, who could blame her? He had asked her out on a date very recently. She felt a sickening sense of disappointment. So his asking her out *had* just been his instinctive reaction to any woman. She should have known. A man like Logan could have his pick. Why would he choose someone who hadn't ever managed to shift the baby weight and whose idea of a great day out was a walk in the park? All the more reason to keep her distance.

'I've known Camilla for longer than I can remember.' Logan broke the silence. 'She was married to my best friend. They're divorced now, but she still calls on me when she needs an escort to some event.'

The thumping sense of relief almost took her breath away. Whatever she was trying to tell herself—it clearly wasn't working. She most definitely wanted Logan not to be involved with another woman—even if she couldn't—shouldn't—have him for herself.

Now, why had he said that? Logan wondered. Especially when it wasn't entirely true. He and Camilla had been lovers once— a long time ago—but as soon as Camilla had known he was back in the UK, she had suggested they take up where they'd left off. He had tried to make it clear as gently and as tactfully as he could that it was over. Yes, she was stunning. Thick dark hair, light green eyes and legs that went on for ever, and she knew it. But what had they ever done together except end up in bed? Once that would have been enough. More than enough. It would have suited him just fine and for the first time he caught himself wondering. When had they shared a joke, gone for a walk, discussed a book? And when had that started to matter? Why did he have the uneasy feeling it had something to do with the woman sitting beside him?

Camilla was as unlike Georgie as it was possible to be, and next to Georgie, Camilla struck him as shallow and self-centred. How come he had never noticed before?

He slid a glance at Georgie who was pointedly staring out of her side window. She wasn't his usual type—too wary for a start. But in Georgie he found it oddly appealing. He wanted to be the one to banish the sadness from eyes the colour of a rain-drenched sky, to bring out the mischievous grin he kept seeing glimpses of. One minute she was daring, the next, he could swear he saw fear in her eyes. What was her story? Back there on the high ropes she had hesitated. Was it his imagination or had she paled? One thing was for sure, she intrigued him. More than any woman he could remember.

Did she have any idea how that rosebud mouth begged to be kissed? How her upturned nose with just a hint of freckles on creamy skin invited touch? He longed to stroke the frown away that appeared too often and press his lips against hers.

Damn it, but he wanted Georgie in his bed. Pity he just didn't do real relationships. And that was the only reason he had refused her invitation. If he allowed himself to be drawn into her family life, who knew what she'd expect from him next? But one thing was for sure—it would be nothing he was prepared to give. He didn't do domesticity, didn't do families, he just did simple, uncomplicated love affairs that were fun. And what was wrong with that? Especially when everything so far in his life had taught him that to love, to get involved, was dangerous.

Logan had managed to find the name of the agency that re-connected adopted children with their parents. Frustratingly, they would only take a name and number from him, promising to give it to his mother if they tracked her down. After that, it would be up to her whether she chose to get in touch. It had

been a few days now and so far nothing. He was beginning to
regret his decision. Why couldn't he let sleeping dogs lie? What
was the point in dragging up the past?

It wasn't as if it would make any difference to his life now.
It wasn't as if he was thinking about a future with another
woman. A future that might involve having a family. No way.
Okay, so he wanted Georgie, but without strings. And why
not? Surely it was time Georgie had fun and where was the
harm in him being the one to remind her? When he took her
out—which he would—it would be somewhere where he could
have her all to himself. It would be a date that would blow her
socks off. Persuading Georgie to have a good time with him was
currently top of his agenda. It would be a challenge and he was
a man who thrived on challenges.

CHAPTER SIX

LATER in the week, Sarah and Georgie met up at Georgie's house to chat over coffee, while their children were playing.

'How's Sibongele getting on?' Georgie asked.

Sarah and Jamie had adopted Sibongele when they'd been in Africa. One of the reasons they had returned to the Glasgow City General had been because Sibongele had been accepted at medical school in the city.

'He's doing well. He loves the course, although he thinks Scotland is too cold.' Sarah smiled. 'I know he misses Africa. Sometimes I miss it too.'

'But you're happy here, aren't you?' Georgie protested. 'How could you not be? You have everything anyone could ever want.'

'Ah, but you know, and I know, it wasn't always like that. Anyway, tell me about you. I can't help noticing that a certain Dr Logan Harris seems to have caught your attention.'

Georgie blushed. 'He is rather gorgeous, isn't he?'

'I couldn't possibly say.' Sarah grinned. 'Me a married woman and all. But let's just say if I hadn't already met and married the man of my dreams, Logan would be in the running.' She drained her coffee cup and sat forward in her chair. 'So tell me, Georgie. What are you going to do about it?'

'Do about it? What do you mean? I'm not going to do anything about it.'

'And why not?' Sarah's eyes softened. 'Isn't it time, Georgie? Anyone can see he's smitten with you.'

Georgie jumped to her feet. 'I....' Then she paused. 'Do you think so? How can you tell?'

Sarah smiled. 'Believe me, I can tell. Hasn't he asked you out yet?'

'Yes,' Georgie admitted, sinking back onto the carpet. She tucked her legs underneath her, knowing it would be a relief to talk to Sarah. 'But I said no.'

Sarah's eyebrows shot up in surprise. 'You said no? Why?'

'Oh, loads of reasons.' She spread her fingers, preparing to reel them off to her friend. 'First, he's not into serious relationships. Trust me. I can tell. Then, he's in the army. I was the child of an army man, and that kind of unsettled existence is not for me or my daughter. Oh, I know some women love it, but I want stability in my life now. Now, where was I? Oh, yes, three. He's in the army and that might have escaped everyone else, but it hasn't escaped me. It's a dangerous, terrible, world out there right now. He could be killed. So that's three very good reasons to have nothing to do with the man. Wouldn't you agree?'

Sarah smiled secretively, as if remembering something. 'I hate to tell you this, Georgie, but some of us have tried to run away from love, only to find it's hopeless. We do it because we're scared. Scared of being hurt usually—I know I was. I also know that sometimes the best thing you can do is face the future with courage, knowing there are no guarantees.' She paused and looked searchingly at Georgie. 'Tell me something. If you had a choice and you could make it right now, knowing that Ian was going to die, what would it be? Would you rather you'd never had that time with him, however short? That you didn't have Jess? Or would you spend every possible minute making the most of the time you had together? Tell me, Georgie, what would you do?'

Later, after Sarah and Calum had left, Georgie read Jess a story, tucked her up in bed then ran herself a bath. She fiddled with the gold band on her left hand. Was Sarah right? Was everyone right? Was it time to get on with her life?

The day Ian had put the ring on her finger came flooding back. It had been snowing. Soft flakes had covered the ground, turning the Scottish scenery into a place of magic. When Ian had slipped the ring onto her finger, it had been the happiest moment of Georgie's life. Little had she known that they'd only have three short years together.

Impulsively she tugged at the ring until with a final twist it was off. Georgie stared down at her now bare hand, noting absent-mindedly that the ring had left a narrow white band on her finger. She went over to her bedside table and opened her jewellery box. She paused for a moment, aware of the significance of the decision she was taking. Her eyes misted with tears as she kissed the ring. 'Goodbye, my love, my heart, I'll never forget you,' she whispered, and gently placed the ring inside the box and closed the lid.

The next few days passed with the usual amount of road traffic accidents and other incidents that were an everyday part of a busy city A and E department.

Often Logan helped out and soon had a reputation in the department of being decisive and innovative in his approach to dealing with casualties, and the department had reason to be grateful he was around when several patients from a nasty accident were brought in.

Fortunately the collision had happened only just over a mile from the hospital. A speeding motorist had crossed the central reservation and flipped onto the other side of the road. Taken by surprise, a young man and his girlfriend travelling on a motorbike had been unable to avoid the car and had crashed into it. The motorbike rider had serious chest injuries as well as several broken limbs. His girlfriend had a head injury while the driver of the car was trapped by the steering wheel of his car and seemed to have breathing difficulties.

Logan arranged for Nick and Lata to attend the scene.

'Nick has the most experience as an anaesthetist. He is best placed to deal with the driver and Lata will be there to assist him. If we went too, we'd only get in the way. Far better we help here,' Logan explained to Georgie.

The A and E team sprang into action. Lizzie telephoned Theatre to ask them to have an emergency team standing by in case they were needed.

It was only ten minutes before the ambulances carrying the injured biker and his girlfriend arrived. Georgie and Logan took the more seriously injured driver while Jamie and Sarah took his girlfriend, who'd been riding pillion.

Although everyone dealt with incidences like this on a regular basis, the injuries to the motorcyclists, as well as their youth, made everyone draw breath. From the odd angle of the young man's foot, his leg had suffered terrible damage in the collision and the injury was bleeding copiously. The biker was conscious but struggling to breathe, and his vital signs suggested that he could be bleeding internally too. They would have to find the bleed and stop it while replacing the fluids he had lost—and quickly. Otherwise there was a very real danger they would lose him.

His girlfriend, although less seriously injured, was also a concern. She was in terrible pain and drifting in and out of consciousness. Georgie knew everyone would do their damnedest to save the young couple's lives.

Georgie cut away the leathers the young man was wearing, knowing that the thick material would have cushioned him somewhat. Nevertheless, she was shocked by what she saw. His foot just above his boot was a mangled mess of skin and bone and jutting out at an abnormal angle. As she checked his vital signs, it seemed something else had caught Logan's eye.

'It's the injuries we can't see that are the most dangerous,' he said, bending over and listening to the patient's chest.

'Breath sounds are okay but look at this imprint on his ribs. It's quite faint but I bet it'll be a massive bruise in a few hours.'

'Pulse 140…BP 72 over 42 …' Georgie called out. It wasn't good. It seemed Logan's instinct had been correct and the young man had a serious internal injury.

'He's quite shocked but we need to get him to CT to check his chest and abdomen. If he's bleeding out into his abdomen, the other injuries don't matter.'

Sure enough, a short while later the duty radiologist confirmed Logan's fear that the man was bleeding from a ruptured spleen.

'Georgie, can you make sure the blood's on its way while I get the surgeons down?' Logan said.

'We've got six units coming but I thought we'd better try to keep one step ahead of the bleeding and give him some O-negative blood. Just look at him, he's as white as a sheet,' she replied, increasingly alarmed at their patient's condition.

'Good thinking. Give him two units stat through the high-speed infuser,' Logan replied, picking up the phone.

Meanwhile, the girlfriend had been much luckier—she only had some head lacerations as well as severe bruising. Sarah and Jamie were preparing to send her to X-Ray to confirm their assessment that she was only concussed.

While everyone had been busy with the motorcyclists, Lata and Nick arrived with the driver of the car that had smashed into the young couple. Lata was sitting on top of his chest, applying CPR, while Nick bagged him. There was a flurry of activity while all spare hands surrounded their patient, attaching him to monitors. Out of the corner of her eye Georgie could see Nick preparing to shock his patient's heart.

Outside Resus, Georgie could hear the cry of a woman in distress and wondered if it was one of the parents. But she couldn't let herself be distracted. They had to get the lad's bleeding under control, and quickly. The initial transfusion had successfully brought up the man's blood pressure and cross-matched blood had arrived too. Lizzie and Georgie applied splints as a temporary measure to the injured limbs and shortly afterwards the surgical team arrived. They agreed with Logan's opinion that he needed to go to Theatre immediately, and set about preparing to transfer the young man.

Nick and Lata were still attempting to resuscitate their patient. From their terse words, Georgie gleaned that they thought that the driver of the car had had a heart attack while driving his car.

Suddenly there was a cry of satisfaction from Nick. 'We have a rhythm. Page the cardiology team.'

Although she knew it was early days yet, Georgie felt incredibly proud to be part of the effort. With everyone working together, utilising the best of their skills, all the patients had the best possible chance.

As soon as the patients were out of their hands Logan stripped off his paper gown and gloves and, tossing them into the bin, indicated with a nod of his head that Georgie follow him.

Outside, Lizzie introduced two couples as the parents of the injured teenagers.

One of the mothers raised a tear-stained face while the other parents stood by, looking too frightened to ask.

Logan crouched by the side of the first couple—the parents of the boy.

'I'm Dr Logan, one of the consultants. Are you the parents of the young man?' His voice was soft.

The woman nodded. 'Is he all right? *Please* tell me he's going to be okay?' She got to her feet as her son was wheeled out on his way to the operating theatre. She made to follow but Logan stopped her.

'Your son has made it this far. That's good. We need to get him to Theatre so the surgeons can remove his spleen.' The woman cried out and sank to the floor.

'It's not as bad as it sounds,' he said quickly. 'Most of us can live perfectly happily without a spleen and your son is a strong young man.'

'What about my daughter?' the other woman interrupted through frozen lips.

'They'll be taking her up to the ward shortly.' Logan said. 'She'll probably be in for a couple of nights, but I think she's going to be just fine.'

The man next to her stepped forward towards the male patient's father.

'I told her she couldn't go on that bike,' he said furiously. 'What kind of parent lets their child own a motorcycle?'

In a flash, Logan placed himself between the two men.

'It wasn't his fault. There was nothing he could have done to avoid hitting the car. We'll know more when the police have finished their investigation, but from what we've been told it was the car driver who caused the accident. It seems he blacked out at the wheel.'

The man looked around wildly, desperate to unleash his

pent-up feelings, needing someone to blame. 'Where is he? That driver. Let me get my hands on him.'

Once again Logan blocked his path. 'The driver is having emergency treatment. As I said, there will be a full police investigation in due course. I can't tell you too much about him without breaking confidentiality, but believe me when I say it wasn't anything he could help.'

The distraught father made to shove Logan out of the way. Georgie couldn't really blame him. He was clearly terrified and this was the only way he knew how to deal with his fear.

Logan stopped him with a gentle but firm grip. 'You can't go in there, I'm afraid. The best thing you can do is wait until they have your daughter settled in the ward and go and see her for yourself.' The man sagged visibly, the fight gone out of him.

'She's my wee girl, my baby,' he said, his voice cracking. 'I can't let anything happen to her.'

'She's going to be all right,' Georgie said quietly. 'You can trust that Dr Harris is telling you the truth.' She looked at him steadily, willing him to believe her. Whatever the father saw in her face seemed to reassure him and he allowed his wife to gather him sobbing into her arms where they comforted each other.

'I'll take you to the relatives' room near Theatre,' Georgie told the other couple. 'You can wait there. Someone will come and speak to you as soon as they've finished operating.'

She left Logan consoling the other parents. When she returned he was at the nurses' station, writing up notes. He looked up when he saw her and gave her a rueful smile.

'Some morning,'

'At least we didn't lose anyone, but for a moment back there I thought it was close.'

'It's a good team here,' Logan said. 'Everyone works well together. It makes a difference.'

'In many ways we're like a little family. It gets to the stage where we know what each other is thinking.'

Logan looked bleak.

'Just like me and my army colleagues,' he said. 'Most of us would lay down our lives for each other, and in some cases have.'

Georgie reached out and touched the scar on his face before she could help herself. 'Have you lost friends?' she asked gently. 'Is that how you got this?'

Logan said nothing. Gently he removed her hand, before staring into the distance for a moment. Then he seemed to recollect himself.

'I don't like to talk about it, if you don't mind. I find it's better just to get on with life and think about the living.' He moved away, forcing Georgie to drop her hand.

'Sometimes it's better to talk, Logan,' she said softly.

He looked at her and for a moment she saw something in his eyes that made her draw a sharp breath. Was it anger? Pain? Regret? Guilt even?

'As I said, it's the living that matter. The here and now. It's all we have and we should make the most of it while we can. Don't you agree?'

'So people keep telling me,' Georgie replied. 'But it's not so easy, is it?'

'But we have to try, don't we?' He glanced around. There was no one within earshot.

'Try with me, Georgie.' His voice was low. 'Come out with me. Just once. And if it doesn't meet your expectations, I won't ask again. Come on,' he urged as she hesitated. 'Take a risk.'

Georgie felt the fight go out of her. 'Why not?' she said. 'You're right. What's there to lose?'

Except my heart, she thought as Logan smiled.

'Until Saturday,' he said, and then he was gone.

CHAPTER SEVEN

SATURDAY arrived clear and warm. Jess woke Georgie up at the crack of dawn and once they'd had breakfast Georgie set about getting ready. Deciding what to wear was a problem. Logan had been cagey when saying where he was taking her. All he had said was to dress comfortably and that they would be having dinner later. Georgie wondered what he had in mind.

Eventually, she settled on a pair of comfortable but smart trousers and a blouse. Hopefully that would see her through most eventualities, but just in case she popped a dress and her favourite cashmere cardigan into her oversized handbag. She knew enough about Logan to suspect that the date would be different.

Her stomach churned. A date. The first she had gone on since Ian. He had been the only serious boyfriend she'd had and they had gone out for years before eventually marrying. Her heart twisted. It felt so disloyal to his memory. When he had died her soul had splintered into a million pieces. If it hadn't been for Jess she thought she might have curled into a ball and never recovered. But the demands of looking after a nine-month-old baby was probably the only reason she had coped. It had left little time for self-pity. Jess needed her. And so every day Georgie had dragged herself out of bed and forced a smile on her face and cared for her daughter. And slowly, so slowly, the terrible pain had begun to ease, until she thought of Ian only once or twice a day, instead of constantly. Sometimes, when Jess turned her head a certain way, or smiled, she would see Ian, and she'd feel a fresh stab of grief. She hoped he'd be happy that she was beginning to make a new life for herself.

Downstairs in the kitchen, her mother was reading the newspaper. She looked up when she heard her daughter.

'Okay, *mo ghràigh*?' she asked.

Georgie poured herself a mug of coffee and sat down next to her mother.

'Am I doing the right thing, Mum?'

Mary peered over the rim of her cup. 'Darling, it's been more than two years. Ian would want you to get on with your life. You know that.'

'It feels wrong. As if I'm forgetting about him.' She glanced down at her hand, at the white band where her wedding ring used to be.

'You'll never forget him. How could you when you were together for so long and have so many happy memories? And you have his child. Part of him lives on in her.'

The two women looked at Jess who was on the kitchen floor bent over her colouring book, her little tongue caught between her lips as she concentrated.

'She looks more and more like Ian every day,' Georgie murmured. She sighed and drained her cup. 'I don't know what I'm getting so het up about. It's only a date. But, Mum, I can't help thinking I'm about to make a big mistake. Maybe I should just call the whole thing off.'

'Whatever for?'

'Because Logan reminds me too much of Ian. He has the same recklessness that Ian had. It scares me. And then there's his career. Supposing anything came of this, then what? I can't see myself as an army wife. Always moving around and living in fear that he might not come back.'

'His job doesn't involve danger, does it? I mean, he's a doctor. Surely they work behind enemy lines?'

Georgie glanced at her watch. 'Grief. Is that the time? He'll be here any minute.' She got up from the table and, bending, kissed her mother on the cheek. 'I'm getting way ahead of myself, Mum. It's too late to back out now. And as I keep telling myself, it's just a date. I suspect that if Logan caught a whiff of something more serious, I wouldn't see him for dust.' She looked across at her daughter. 'Somehow I don't see him as a family man. I'm just going to take the date at face value and have some fun.' She stretched. 'It's been a very long time since I had any.'

Her mother smiled back. 'So isn't it about time you did? God knows, everyone, most of all you, has the right to be happy. We have to find happiness wherever and whenever we can. You know that more than most, Georgie. Life is short.'

Mary's eyes misted and Georgie knew she was thinking about her father. She bent and kissed her mother's cheek, hugging her fiercely.

'Wish me luck, Mum,' Georgie said, hearing the sound of a car pulling up outside. 'I've got the strangest feeling I'm going to need it.'

Georgie was out the door and by the car before Logan had time to get out. She didn't want Jess to get any more attached to Logan than she already was. Not until she knew where, if anywhere, this was going. On the other hand, rushing out like that must make her look embarrassingly keen to Logan. Cripes. When she had wanted to seem impossibly cool. She sighed inwardly. He would just have to think what he liked. Explanations would only make matters worse.

'All set?' Logan grinned, his eyes creasing at the corners. Georgie's pulse did that curious hippity-hop it always did these days when he smiled.

'You still haven't said where we're going,' she remarked, dumping her handbag in the back seat.

'No, I didn't, did I?' Logan said obliquely. 'If I did, it wouldn't be a surprise.'

As they headed out of Glasgow, Georgie sat back, enjoying the feel of the wind in her hair. It was the first time in years she'd felt carefree and she was determined to enjoy every minute of her day out. For once she was going forget about responsibility and put herself in someone else's hands. And as for the future? Who cared? She had done enough worrying about that to last a lifetime.

They chatted about music as they drove. He liked jazz, she hated it. She loved opera and he hated it. Surprisingly they both agreed on 1970s rock. Then they discussed books. He rarely read, but when he did it was biographies. She read whenever she could and devoured thrillers.

'I've enough real-life thrills in my life, without having to read about them.' He smiled but Georgie thought she saw sadness flit across his eyes, though it was gone before she could be sure. 'Besides, there's not much time to read. Training for the pentathlon keeps me busy when I'm not working.'

'How do you train?' Georgie asked, genuinely curious.

'It depends where I am. While I'm in Glasgow I go for a run on the hills most mornings before work. After work I go to the pool and swim a mile or two.'

'A mile or two!' Georgie spluttered. 'Tell me you're kidding! The last time I went swimming I only managed about five lengths before I was a heaving wreck.'

Logan slid a look in her direction. 'You seem pretty fit to me.'

She blushed under his obvious admiration and shifted uncomfortably in her seat. 'I was once. When I climbed regularly.
But since I had Jess…' She shrugged. 'There never seems to
be enough hours in the day. I work. I look after my daughter,
tidy up, shop, cook. And by the time I've done all that, I'm
ready for bed.' God, now she sounded as if she was complain-
ing when her life had everything she wanted. Or so she kept
telling herself.

'That's why I don't think I'll ever have kids.' Although his
tone was light, Georgie had the distinct impression he wanted
to make sure she knew he wasn't into offering her a future. 'I'm
too selfish, I guess. Too used to pleasing myself.'

Georgie felt a crunch of disappointment. The message was
loud and clear. But, then, hadn't she just being telling herself
she wasn't interested in a long-term relationship with this man
either? She certainly wasn't even thinking of the future. Besides, it seemed that they had little in common, except perhaps
a love of medicine. Any attraction she felt for him was purely
physical, the result surely of almost three years of celibacy? A
warmth spread from low in her abdomen. Sex. It had been a
long time since she had even thought about it. But with this man
she was having a hard time thinking of anything else! Thank
God, he couldn't read minds. But when he turned and grinned
at her she began to have her doubts. She could have sworn from
the way his eyes were glinting that he had heard every thought
as clearly as if she had shouted it.

They drew up in what seemed to be a large empty car park
in the middle of nowhere. Georgie was completely baffled.
She had imagined a walk in the hills, a trip to Loch Lomond
perhaps, lunch somewhere—but this?

All she could see was what looked like an empty Nissen hut
and way over on the other side a number of small private planes.

As realisation began to dawn, her heart thumped painfully. Not a plane trip, please, God. And certainly not in one of these tin cans.

But it seemed that was exactly what Logan had in mind.

'There's a hotel on an island about an hour's flight from here, where they have a great restaurant. You can only reach the hotel by boat or plane—it has its own private landing strip. And as I have to keep up my flying hours, I thought it the perfect place for our first date.'

Stunned, Georgie only barely registered his use of the word *first*. What was she going to do? She could cope with the helicopter, but this was different. This was tiny and she would be unable to pretend she wasn't miles above the ground. She could hardly admit she was terrified at the thought of going up in the two-seater. Logan would have serious doubts about her suitability for the emergency rescue team if she did. On the other hand, she could hardly disguise her fear for the whole journey, there and back. Oh, God, she had the way back to think about too! The whole date thing was turning into a nightmare. Why, oh, why had she agreed to come? There was nothing wrong with the life she had made for herself. Until she had met Logan she had been content, *and* she hadn't been constantly challenged.

'But before we leave I've arranged for a tandem skydive.'

This time Georgie's heart sank to her boots. No way. No way at all was she going to go up in a plane to throw herself into space. He would have to drug her first and wait until she was unconscious before flinging her out. That would teach her to fancy action men. From now on the only men she would date were those whose idea of excitement was a walk in the rain.

Then she realised Logan was laughing at her. 'I'm only kidding. About the skydiving. At least, today.' He laid a hand gently on her shoulder and pulled her round to face him. He lifted her chin with his finger.

'You're shaking,' he said. 'Do you want to tell me why?'

Georgie shook her head.

'You don't like planes, do you?' he said quietly. It wasn't a question. 'But you can cope with helicopters?'

Relief made her knees weak. It was better that he knew.

'I don't mind helicopters so much, because I can't see where we're going. I can make myself believe that I'm still on the ground. But for some reason, the thought of going up in a small plane makes me feel sick. I think it's because…' She bit back the words.

'Because?' Logan prompted gently.

'Because I spent two days in a light aircraft helping to look for my husband's body,' she blurted. 'Now I can't go near one without reliving the whole awful experience. Especially not small ones, like those.' She pointed at the row of planes sitting on the tarmac.

He squeezed her hand and she saw sympathy in his eyes. 'You should have told me. Perhaps I could have helped. '

'And have you think twice about having me on the team?' She shook her head. 'I can cope with the helicopter. That's what matters, isn't it?'

'But we may have to go with the air ambulance plane at some point. And what if your anxiety spreads to the helicopter? We're bound to find ourselves in some hairy conditions sometime. I'm sorry, Georgie. I wish you had said. I can't afford to have someone on the team who could crack at any time.' He looked genuinely regretful.

Georgie swallowed hard. There was no way she was going to give up her place on the team. She had never failed at anything and she was damned if she was going to start now. Hadn't she just resolved to face the future without fear?

She stiffened her spine and faced him. The last thing she wanted was for anyone, especially this man, to see her as a wimp.

'If I can cope with the plane trip, there and back, will you keep me on the team?'

Logan studied her for one long moment. 'One condition. If it becomes unbearable—before it becomes unbearable—you'll let me know.'

Georgie raised her hand in a mock salute and managed a smile. 'Aye, aye, sir. Hadn't we better get going, then?'

Her heart was in her mouth the whole time Logan did his checks. The plane was tiny, with just enough room for the pair of them, and of course she would be unable to avoid looking out unless she kept her eyes closed the whole time. Impossible. Not without eagle-eyed Logan noticing. She was pretty sure he wouldn't be satisfied that she had kept her part of the bargain if she did. Cripes. If she had known what he had in mind she would have stopped off for some mild sedatives. But that wasn't the answer either. No. There was nothing else for it. She would have to grit her teeth and pray.

The worst part was taking off. A wave of nausea brought tiny beads of perspiration to her top lip.

'You have strong fingers,' Logan said wryly as soon as they were airborne. Abashed, she whipped her hand off his thigh, but not before she was conscious of steel-like muscles under her fingertips.

'Years of climbing, I guess,' she said trying hard to keep her voice light. She hadn't been aware she had clutched his thigh. One more embarrassment to add to a steadily growing list.

Logan pointed out various landmarks and soon Georgie found that she was beginning to relax. At least, enough for the nausea to pass.

As the flight went on, Georgie felt the tension ease. Soon she was able to peer out of the window. They flew over Loch

Lomond and seemed to be following the coastline. Below, she could make out tiny boats and yachts as they sailed into the sea.

Twenty minutes later, they started their descent towards a small island. The sea was cobalt blue, lightening where the water became more shallow near the fringes of the island. The sky was cloudless and Georgie felt relaxed.

Nevertheless she was relieved when they touched down with hardly a bump. Now she only had the return journey to get through. She knew she had all but conquered her fear. Perhaps if she had forced herself to fly sooner, she wouldn't have had those years of worrying, wondering if she'd ever be able to take Jess overseas on holiday. Fear, she realised, was worse in the imagination than reality.

As the plane came to a halt, they removed their helmets. Logan looked at her expectantly. 'Well?' he asked.

'It wasn't nearly as awful as I imagined it would be,' Georgie admitted. 'In fact, towards the end I was beginning to enjoy myself. It's such a relief. I hated being scared.'

'There's nothing wrong with being frightened,' he said softly. 'It's what keeps us safe. It's how you cope with that fear that counts.'

Georgie wondered if he were talking from personal experience. She wanted to know more, but instinctively knew that now wasn't the right time.

The hotel was perched on a cliff overlooking the sea. Despite its remote and inaccessible location, the restaurant was busy. Georgie suspected that many of the boats tied up in the harbour used it as a stopping-off point on their journey up the west coast.

'I've heard of this place,' she said appreciatively. 'Never thought I'd come here, though.'

Logan had arranged the hire of a small boat and organised a picnic for their lunch.

'There's a small deserted island just over there.' He pointed to a small chunk of land out at sea. 'I thought we could take the boat across, have lunch and then go for a walk.'

Georgie had to admit he had picked a perfect day weather-wise. The sun glinted on the sea, turning it to rippled silver. There was a hint of rain to come in the distance, but it would be some time before it reached them.

Logan insisted on rowing across and Georgie was happy to let him. This way she could relax while watching him surrep-titiously. He rowed effortlessly, his muscles bunching with the effort. All Georgie could think about was how it would feel to have those arms wrapped around her, holding her tight, and her stomach fluttered nervously.

During their picnic and walk, Logan amused her with stories about his days in the territorial army and boot camp, as well as describing a few of the places he had been posted to during his career. She noticed he kept away from talking about his current posting. She could hardly blame him. He would be going back there soon enough. In turn, she told him about some of the fas-cinating places her father had been posted to. Talking about them made her realise that her dislocated childhood hadn't been all bad. She had seen and done things she would never have done had her father not been in the army.

The hours sped by and before she knew it they were rowing back towards the main island.

'This has been wonderful, Logan. Thank you,' Georgie said, leaning back and raising her face to the gentle sun.

'It needn't be over yet.' He hesitated and for the first time he looked unsure of himself. 'I made dinner reservations for us at the hotel. But if you'd rather go back…'

She trailed a languid hand in the cool water. She liked seeing this other, less sure side of him. It made him seem more human.

'Leave paradise before I have to? No way. Dinner sounds lovely.' Georgie was glad she had tucked an emerald green wraparound dress into her bag in case her date had required something more dressy. She slipped it on in the hotel rest room, refreshed her make-up, brushed her hair until it gleamed and sprayed some perfume on her wrists and neck before joining Logan in the foyer. He let out an appreciative wolf whistle when he saw her.

'You look beautiful,' he said as she walked towards him. 'I wish I had brought something more formal.' However, he looked completely relaxed and at ease in his jeans and T-shirt.

Their meal more than lived up to its reputation. Georgie had warm pigeon breast to start with then they shared a platter of seafood. It wasn't the most elegant dish to eat, but they both tucked in with gusto.

'Here, try a whelk,' Georgie said, holding out a tiny morsel of the shellfish.

'Think I'll pass.' Logan said, wrinkling his nose.

'Oh, no, you don't.' Georgie laughed. 'I had to do something I didn't want to today, so fair's fair. Now it's your turn.'

She wiggled the whelk under his nose and Logan obediently opened his mouth to accept her offering. He chewed thoughtfully for a moment before swallowing. 'Not bad. Not great either, but not bad. Now you.' He held out an oyster. Georgie had been avoiding those particular molluscs.

'Sorry, don't do raw shellfish.' Georgie shook her head. 'Anyway, aren't they supposed to be aphrodisiacs?'

As soon as the words were out of her mouth, she could have bitten her tongue. Logan smiled slowly. God, he had the sexiest smile. And the way he was looking at her… All of a sudden she felt hot and flustered. It didn't take a magician to work out what he was thinking.

He reached across the table and cupped her jaw in his hand. She shivered as she felt his fingers on her throat. Heat flooded her body, leaving her breathless.

'Close your eyes and open your mouth.' His voice was low, husky, and time stood still. The other diners receded and she and Logan could have been alone. Unable to stop herself, she closed her eyes and parted her lips. He dropped the oyster into her mouth, and she tasted salt, then the sea, then the unusual feel of the icy shellfish on her tongue.

'Now swallow,' he instructed. His voice felt as if it was coming from a million miles away. She did as she was told. The oyster left a strange, not unpleasant aftertaste and she opened her eyes.

Logan grinned with delight when she gave a nod of approval and her heart stuttered.

They chatted while they finished their meal, keeping the conversation on neutral ground. When they were offered dessert, Georgie declined regretfully, thinking of the weight she planned to lose. The last thing she wanted was for her fitness to be called into question too. At one time she would have been able to run up Dumgoyne outside Glasgow without stopping. Now she doubted she could walk up it without catching her breath. Time for some serious training.

Logan was tucking enthusiastically into a plate of cheese and oatcakes. Clearly *he* didn't have an issue with weight. Every inch of his body was streamlined perfection. A languorous warmth spread through her lower body as she imagined herself pressed against him. Not once since Ian had died had she felt even the slightest attraction for another man, yet here she was almost salivating over this one.

'Tell me about Ian,' he said suddenly, as if he could read her mind.

Georgie bit her lip. She didn't want to think about Ian right now, let alone talk about him. For the past few hours she had felt safe in a bubble where nothing else mattered but being in the moment with this man, and she wanted to stay right where she was, where death and loss and guilt and fear didn't exist. And she did feel guilt. As if she were being unfaithful to Ian. In her heart, she knew she had taken another step towards a future without him. First putting away her wedding ring and then this date, and although Logan wasn't offering her a future with him, she was in no doubt that he wanted her. But for how long? Days? Weeks? Months?

Across the table Logan was watching her intently. 'You don't have to tell me,' he said gently. 'Just tell me it's none of my business.' His eyes were warm as he looked at her. 'We can talk about something else.'

Outside, the day had darkened and spots of rain tapped against the window. The waiter came across and lit a candle.

No, Georgie wasn't ready to talk about Ian. Not here. Not now. She preferred to remain cocooned, forgetting about the past and not thinking about the future. Why couldn't he pretend with her that nothing else existed except the two of them and the here and now?

'The weather is getting worse,' she said.

He followed her gaze to the window. A splatter of rain suddenly hurled itself against the glass.

'If we're going, we should go now.'

If. He had said if. The atmosphere between them intensified. It was electric, sizzling with possibilities.

'We could stay and go back tomorrow…' Logan said, his eyes drilling into hers.

There was a tightness in her chest and she was having difficulty breathing normally.

'What about Jess?' she whispered.

'Phone home.'

Two simple words and her world stood still. She didn't even pretend not to understand what he was suggesting.

Logan reached across the table and touched her cheek. Her skin felt as if a thousand tiny sparks were flitting across it. Georgie knew she couldn't leave. And she didn't want to.

Unable to speak, she nodded.

Logan stood, his eyes darkening. 'You phone,' he said. 'I'll see if they have a room.'

Her heart racing, Georgie rang home. Her mother answered and after discovering that Jess was in bed already, Georgie asked if she would mind looking after her until the next day.

There was a silence at the other end of the phone.

'Do you know what you're doing, love?' her mother asked quietly. 'I know I said it's about time you got on with your life, but I didn't mean to jump in feet first.'

'Not really, Mum. But I'm going to anyway.'

'Jess will be fine with me,' her mother said at last. 'You take care.'

Logan returned to her side.

'They have a room. Overlooking the sea.' Once more his dark eyes stared into hers. 'You can still change your mind.'

Wordlessly, Georgie shook her head. Logan took her hand and together they made their way out of the hotel.

'They've given us a room in the boathouse, looking out over the beach.' Logan explained. 'It's separate from the hotel, but has the best view.'

Somehow Georgie didn't think they'd be worrying about the view.

As the rain began to fall in earnest they ran the few yards to the boathouse.

Logan opened the door and pulled her into his arms, kicking the door closed behind him.

Georgie was shivering, though whether from the cold or fear she couldn't be sure. But then his mouth was on hers.

The kiss was just how she'd imagined it would be. Firm yet soft. Demanding yet gentle. Heat flooded her body as she moulded herself to him, feeling the hard muscles of his chest and thighs pressing against her body.

He dropped his hands to her hips and tugged her even closer. She kissed him hungrily and the outside world disappeared.

But when he moved to undo the ties of her dress, she stiffened. Involuntarily, she halted his hands, placing hers on top of his.

He became still. 'Georgie?' His eyes glinted down at her. 'You're not sure? It's okay. We don't have to.'

She shook her head and pressed a finger against his mouth. 'Could we put the lights out?'

He looked bewildered. 'If you like. But why? I want to look at you. Every scrap of you.'

'Baby weight,' Georgie muttered, feeling ridiculous.

He threw back his head and laughed. 'But don't you know how gorgeous you are? I love your curves. Your sexy, womanly curves.' He dropped kisses on her shoulder as he slid the dress from her shoulders.

Slowly. Ever so slowly, his eyes not leaving hers, he undid the ties of her dress, and she let it slide to the floor.

She shivered again as he dropped a kiss on the swell of each breast.

Then he slid the straps of her bra down her shoulders and unhooked it. As her breasts sprang free she resisted the impulse to cover herself with her arms, feeling shy again. She had never made love to anyone apart from Ian and no other man— bar her doctor—had ever seen her naked. What if she didn't know how to please him? What if he was put off by her post-baby figure?

He sat down on the bed and pulled her closer so she was standing between his legs. Then he peeled off his T-shirt, revealing a tanned, muscular chest. Every muscle was clearly perfectly defined, his upper arms evidence of a man whose body was used to daily hard physical activity.

Finally he eased her satin slip over her hips. It slithered onto the floor. Now she was standing before him naked except for her panties. Any reservations she'd had melted away when she saw the look in his eyes and knew he found her beautiful.

His thumbs followed a lazy path over her hip bones and his lips traced a path along her abdomen until eventually they found her breasts. He took each nipple in his mouth in turn, teasing with his tongue until Georgie moaned with the pleasure of it.

'You take my breath away, Georgie McArthur,' he said against her skin, and she knew it would be all right.

As if unable to stop himself, he gathered her onto his lap and, falling backwards on the bed, rolled her beneath him, raining kisses on her face and body. She ached to be closer to him. She fumbled at the button of his jeans but her fingers couldn't get a grip because she could not stop herself from pressing against him. Reluctantly, it seemed, he tore himself away from her and slipped a hand into his jeans pocket and pulled out a condom.

She drank him in, admiring the long, lean length of his legs as he yanked off his jeans and boxers. Seconds later, he was beside her again. His legs were long with powerful thighs, his desire for her evident.

Teasingly, he brushed his hands up the inner part of her thigh until every nerve ending was on fire. Then at last, almost when she couldn't bear it any longer, he hooked his fingers under the lace at the top of her panties and eased them down.

Georgie closed her eyes. She heard him groan as he lifted himself off her again for a few agonising seconds. When she heard the wrapper rip, she knew he was protecting them both.

Then his hands were all over her again and she responded, revelling in the hardness of him under her fingertips, his male scent. Just when she thought she could bear it no more, that she would explode with her need for him, he parted her legs and was inside her.

Much later they lay in each other's arms, sated. The rain lashed outside, but lying in the circle of Logan's arms Georgie felt safe and at peace. She trailed her fingertips across his chest and down towards his abdomen to where the dark hair was thicker. Propping herself on her elbow, she followed the touch of her hands with small kisses, ever downwards.

He moaned and wrapped his hand in her hair. Then once more they lost themselves in each other.

Later still, as they lay listening to the rain in a tangle of sheets, Georgie started to talk.

'It happened three years ago,' she began. Suddenly she was back in that dreadful, horrific night.

Logan stroked her hair, waiting for her to continue.

'Ian, Jess's father, my husband…' she swallowed hard '…was a member of the mountain rescue team based in Fort William. We both were. That's how we met.' She smiled, remembering Ian's cheeky grin and how he'd refused to take no for an answer when he'd asked her out. 'We both loved the mountains. Both of us had spent most of our lives climbing and there was nothing either of us loved more. We often went on rescues together, kind of watching each other's backs, you know. Kirk didn't really like it that we were both on the team. He thought it might cause one of us to make a bad decision to protect the other.'

'Go on,' he said gently.

Georgie wrapped herself in the sheet and perched on the end of the bed.

'Ian just laughed. He told Kirk that it was more likely I would have to rescue him than the other way round. He said I was like a cat on the mountains.' A familiar stab of loss jarred her heart, but as he tugged her gently back down beside him and cradled her in his arms, the telling became easier.

'We were together for a few years before we got married— we were busy with our careers. He was a doctor at the hospital at Fort William where I worked as a nurse and we continued to climb and go out with the mountain rescue team. We had some scary moments but we always managed, with the rest of the team, to come through. There was something very fulfilling about helping people who shared our love of the mountains. But we didn't—couldn't—always save everyone. People always underestimate the mountains in Scotland. There is at least one death every winter, sometimes more. And sometimes in the summer too. The days can seem so benign that climbers and walkers don't recognise the danger. Of course, we understood the risks involved in the rescues, but we had confidence in our ability and each other. And loving the mountains as we did, we could never blame folk for wanting to be out there. I guess it must be like that for people in the army too.'

A shadow crossed Logan's face. 'I know what you're saying,' he said heavily. 'Most join the army because they love the life. They know they put their lives in danger everyday when they are in a war zone and they do it without hesitation to help their fellow soldiers. The bravery and courage of these men is humbling. But there are some who don't really appreciate the danger until they are out there. The reality of shooting at live targets and being shot at. And even when they do, they stay because they feel it is their duty. Then there are the NHS volunteers, ordinary men and women who put their lives on hold for months so that they can be there to help wherever they are needed. I have met some of the bravest men and women I know in the army.' The desolate look in his eyes was back. Georgie wanted to banish it, the same way he had banished her loneliness.

'It must make my fear seem very trivial,' Georgie said feeling a little ashamed.

'As I said earlier, the really brave people are those who feel fear yet face it anyway. Those who never feel fear are a rare breed—or crazy.' He touched her arm, letting his long fingers trail down to her hand. Her skin burned where he touched her. She smiled at him.

'Like you? I can't imagine you being scared of anything.'

Logan grinned. 'Believe me, there are situations that frighten the hell out of me. But we were talking about you.'

'Jess came along after we'd been married for a couple of years. Obviously when I was heavily pregnant I had to stop climbing, let alone going out on rescues. In fact, Kirk and Ian stopped me going out on rescues as soon as they knew I was pregnant.' She shook her head, remembering well how cross she had been at first, until she'd realised that they were right. The more the other members of the team worried about her, the more she'd be putting everyone's life at risk.

'Then, of course, having a small baby made it equally impossible. And strangely enough the first time I climbed after Jess's birth, I began to feel nervous. I think it must be something to do with being a mother. It's as if you know your child needs you alive or something.'

Logan pulled her down beside him and turned on his side. There faces were barely inches apart and she could feel his warm breath on her skin. He looked at her intently. It was as if he knew she was coming to the hard part.

'One winter, just before Jess's first Christmas, the team got a call. Two ice climbers hadn't returned from their climb. It was dark and there was a weather front moving in. They had been advised against the climb by locals earlier in the day, but they didn't listen.' Her eyes closed as the memory of that day rushed back in excruciating detail.

'To cut a long story short, Ian went out with the team. Kirk was leading, of course. Although the weather had worsened they thought they would have enough time to get to the ice waterfall where the men were climbing.' Georgie sucked in a painful breath.

'But the weather turned to blizzard conditions much sooner than anyone expected. Ian lost his footing, no one knows how, and went over the side. Kirk and the rest of the team tried to reach him, but no matter how they tried they couldn't even see him. The weather was too bad for the RAF to help. There was nothing else for it but to wait until daybreak to try again.' Georgie's throat felt as if it was being sliced with razor blades. She remembered every minute of that long night. The slow ticking of the clock. Wondering if Ian was injured, alive even and slowly freezing to death. Kirk had refused to leave the mountain, saying he couldn't leave Ian alone, and she and her mother had worried about him too. That night Georgie hadn't known whether she was going to lose a husband and a brother.

'The waiting was the worst part. As soon as it was light, the team went out again, and the weather had cleared sufficiently for the RAF to send a helicopter. They wouldn't take me, so I made someone I knew take me out in their light plane. I think I swore and screamed. Anything to make him take me.' She paused, taking a moment to moisten her lips.

'As soon as I could, I was on the plane, searching along with everyone else. Hoping to catch a glimpse of his red jacket in the snow. But a couple of inches had fallen overnight and if Ian was out there, we just couldn't find him.' This time she couldn't help the tears from falling as she remembered those desperate hours, knowing that every minute that passed made the possibility of finding him alive more remote.

Logan watched her steadily, not saying anything. Only the pressure of his fingers on the small of her back told her he was aware of her pain.

'We found him eventually. Two days later. Dead. The only consolation was finding out his neck was broken. He must have died instantly, so even if we'd got to him straight away, it wouldn't have made any difference.' She laughed bitterly. 'Some consolation, huh? My daughter would never know her father. And as for the climbers he had set out to rescue, they were found alive and well, having taken shelter in a bothy. Oh, I don't blame them, I don't blame anyone. I was mad with grief and mad with the world at first, but Mum made me realise I owed it to Jess to pull myself together so that's what I did. I guess my fear of small planes is rooted in the fear I felt as we looked for him. It just became associated with small aircraft, the way these things do.'

He hugged her closer. 'I am so sorry, Georgie. That must have been hard.'

She managed a smile. 'The toughest couple of years of my life. I still miss him. I miss him when Jess is sick, or when she does something new. I find myself thinking, I wonder what Ian will think? Then it hits me all over again. But it is getting easier. People tell you when it first happens that time will heal and you can't believe them, but it does. I find myself remembering the good times and smiling. I'll never forget him, but it's time to move on. In many ways the new service we've been setting up has been a godsend. It's given me something to look forward to.' A ring of ice circled her heart as she said the words. What if Logan took her off the team? What if he decided her fear was too much of a risk?

'And now? How do you feel about being in a small aircraft now?'

'I think the fear of the fear was worse—if that makes sense?'

Logan nodded slowly. 'It will probably take a few trips before it goes completely, but I reckon you'll be okay.'

Georgie relaxed, not even realising she'd been holding her breath.

'Does that mean I'm still on the team?'

'I can't think of anyone else I'd rather have.' But as she smiled her relief he held up a hand. 'But I'm warning you, if at any time I think your fear is getting the better of you, you're off. I wouldn't want to do it, but if I thought the safety of the team was being compromised, I'd do it in a flash.'

Georgie nodded. Then she held out her hand. 'It's a deal,' she said.

Logan listened to the rhythmic sound of Georgie's breathing. He was shocked at the way this woman had crept under his skin. He had meant it to be a casual affair, something to pass the time until he was called back to the army, but now he knew he had been fooling himself.

She wasn't his typical woman. Mostly he sought women out who wanted as little from him as he was prepared to give, and that suited him fine. But Georgie was different. She had opened her heart to him, let him see her vulnerability, her fear and, ultimately, her courage.

He suppressed a groan. This wasn't what he had intended.

To become involved with a woman who could no more pretend to be something she wasn't than he could walk on water. This was no casual affair for her. He was the first man she had slept with since her husband and that meant responsibility. What was he going to do?

He knew one thing for sure. He didn't want to let her go. Maybe Georgie could fill that missing place in his heart? The place that had been empty since he'd been two years old and his mother had left him. Maybe Georgie was what he had been waiting for all his life, without even knowing it?

He recoiled from the thought. Marriage. Responsibility. A ready-made family. Could he do it? Did he even have it in him? He hadn't been joking when he had told her that he was frightened of certain things. What she didn't know was that it was commitment. Family life. Settling down. There wasn't anything physically that frightened him as much as these words. What if he couldn't stick it? What if he was like his mother?

A couple of days ago she had rung him back. She had been polite but distant. She was glad to hear he was okay, but she had married and had a new family. None of them knew about him, and if he didn't mind, could they keep it that way? She was sorry she'd had to give him up, but she had been young and unable to cope. She was sure he would understand.

It hadn't been the conversation he had imagined in his head, but somehow it had helped. How could he really blame her for giving him up? She had been young and alone. He was different. Georgie was different. And there was no way he was going to walk away from Georgie the way his mother had walked away from him. Not now. For once he was going to open his heart and see where it took him. He had to try. For better or for worse.

CHAPTER EIGHT

WHEN Georgie woke up she had no idea at first where she was. Then it all came flooding back. She was here on an island with Logan. And they had made love. Several times. She blushed as the images played out in her head. Turning her head, the empty expanse of the bed told her Logan had already risen.

She slid out of bed, wondering where he had got to. Seeing his discarded shirt on the floor, she slipped it over her head, inhaling the now familiar scent of him, and crossed to the window. Pulling the curtains open, she gasped with pleasure as the bright cloudless sky revealed a snow-white beach that seemed to stretch for miles. She flung the windows open and breathed in the smell of the sea. Waves lapped invitingly on the shore. Perhaps they would have time for a swim before they had to leave?

Making herself a coffee from the hospitality tray, she returned to the window. How would Logan be feeling this morning? Would he already be regretting taking her to bed? Would he be thinking that it compromised their working relationship? She would put him at ease. Right now, this was all she wanted. An interlude in her life. He would leave, she knew that, and that would be okay. She would miss him unbearably, but what was the alternative?

She caught sight of a figure on the beach. It was Logan running, bare-chested and barefoot. Her breath caught in her

throat. Who was she kidding? She had fallen hook, line and
sinker for this enigmatic man. It was as if she had, since Ian's
death, being daydreaming her way through life. Now every
fibre of her being tingled with excitement and a heady joy, and
she didn't ever want to lose that feeling again. She would take
every day with Logan as it came. And if it ended? Well, she
would face that too. Sarah had been right. Far better to experience another wrenching loss than never to have experienced
what the two of them had had last night.

Logan opened the door. His chest was gleaming with perspiration, highlighting each individual muscle, and Georgie
felt her abdomen clench. Forcing herself to remain casual, she
smiled at him, nodding towards the kettle.

'You were up early. Can I get you a coffee?'

Logan was looking at her, his dark eyes alight. Self-
consciously she tugged the shirt down, but Logan took a step
towards her and slipped his hands underneath.

'I'm kind of sweaty after my run,' he murmured in her ear.
'How do you fancy taking a shower with me?' And then,
laughing, they were moving, still clinging to each other, towards
the bathroom, tugging feverishly at each other's clothes.

Much later, it was time for them to leave. Georgie phoned
home to check Jess was okay and to tell her mother they'd be
back for lunch.

'Did you have a good time, darling?' her mother asked softly.

Conscious of Logan watching her, a half-smile on his face,
Georgie blushed to the tips of her toes.

'Yes,' she said softly. 'I'll tell you all about it when I see
you.' Perhaps not *all* about it.

While Georgie was talking to her mother, Logan studied her.
Her red hair was still damp from their shower and her cheeks

glowed after their love-making. Something shifted inside him. He hadn't planned this. Oh, he had wanted to make love to her, almost as soon as he had met her, but he hadn't expected to feel this way. He had never imagined that she would take a hold on his heart. He closed his eyes. Images of their love-making flooded back. The way her body had responded to his, as if they were involved in a dance that only the two of them knew the tune to. And it wasn't just physical attraction either. She was brave and funny and vulnerable and dedicated. Unlike any woman he'd had a relationship with before—if you could call what he'd had before in his life relationships, that was. None of the other woman had made him feel this kind of connection. Not to the extent he felt connected to Georgie. It was as if he'd been looking for her all his life. That she was the missing half of his soul.

What now? This wasn't what he had intended or expected. Last night he'd thought that he would be able to take a chance, open his heart and see what happened, but had that just been the after-effects of the closeness they'd shared? After all, he wasn't into playing happy families and he knew without a shadow of doubt that Georgie wasn't into anything less. He groaned under his breath. Already he was in deeper than he had been before. Perhaps he should call a halt now before he was in over his head? But as Georgie finished her phone call and looked at him mischievously from those spectacular grey-blue eyes, he knew it was too late.

The sun was shining brightly by the time they were in the plane again and Logan was making his preparations for take-off. Out of the corner of her eye, Georgie studied him as he concentrated on his final checks. A rush of happiness flowed through her, followed closely by a shiver of apprehension. What had she done? She could tell herself that it was just a casual fling until the cows came home, but she knew she'd be kidding herself. Somewhere along the way, she had fallen for this man. Fallen hard. And that definitely wasn't in the plan. She had to remember that he was everything she refused to have in her life... No. She was getting way ahead of herself. One night. That was it. And she would have to make sure it stayed that way. Far better to have some pain now then go through heartbreak later on.

As the engines whirled into action, Logan turned to her and flashed his heart-stopping grin.

'Nervous?' he asked, his eyes turning serious

'Not at all,' Georgie replied truthfully. And it was the truth. Her fear of planes had left her, almost as if it had never existed, and in its place was a much deeper fear. Fear of losing someone all over again.

As they drew up in front of her house, Georgie paused, her hand on the passenger door. Would he say anything? Or would they both pretend the night hadn't happened?

'Thank you for coming,' he said formally. 'I had a cool time.'

'So did I,' Georgie replied equally formally.

'Will you come to dinner with me tonight? I hear there's a new restaurant in merchant city that's getting rave reviews.'

Georgie shook her head regretfully. 'I don't think that's a good idea. Apart from anything else, I've just spent a night away from my daughter. It wouldn't be fair to ask Mum to look after her again.' She licked dry lips. She was being evasive when she owed it to him to be direct.

He frowned. 'What about tomorrow night? Or the night after that? Or I can wait until the weekend if you'd prefer? It will be a long week, but I'm a patient man—when I need to be.'

'I don't know. This has taken me by surprise. It's all happened so fast. I think we should step back for a bit.' She touched his hand. 'Give me some time, okay?'

His eyes locked on to hers. She saw surprise there, and determination.

He brought his hand to his forehead in a mock salute. 'Sure thing, ma'am,' he said lightly. 'But I'm not going to give up easily. As long as you understand that.'

CHAPTER NINE

BACK at the hospital, the days passed much as they had done before. To her chagrin—and hurt—Logan treated her as if the night on the island never happened. He was friendly, but no more or less than he was to his other colleagues. What else did she expect? She had told him she didn't want to be rushed, and all he had done was take her at her word. However, she couldn't quite convince herself. Perhaps he was relieved she had pulled away? Perhaps, having had time to reflect, he was glad she had been the one to call a halt?

Whatever. It was better this way. She would get over him. He would move on and she would return to her predictable, happy, safe life.

One afternoon, Lizzie asked if she could have a private word. She took her into the office and closed the door. She waited until Georgie had sat down.

'I haven't really told anyone yet, apart from close friends, but I'm pregnant, Georgie,' Lizzie said, smiling widely.

Georgie jumped up and hugged her. She had guessed that Lizzie would be hoping to start a family sooner than later. 'That's wonderful news! You must be so excited!'

Lizzie's grin grew wider. 'If you think I'm excited, you should see Stewart. He's already bought the cot.'

'How far on are you? Are you feeling okay?'

'I'm just past the twelve-week mark. And, yes, I'm feeling fine. I had a bit of morning sickness early on, but it's settled down now. Obviously I'm going to be taking time off—at least a year, maybe more—and that's why I wanted to talk to you.'

Georgie sat down again. 'I'm all ears.'

'While I'm away, someone will need to step into my shoes as department manager. I thought you might fancy it.'

Georgie was dumbstruck. While Jess was at home, she hadn't really considered where her career was going. The role with the MERT team had been an unexpected challenge. One that she was loving. Maybe once she would have jumped at the chance. Now she wasn't so sure.

'I don't know, Lizzie. At one time I would have grabbed the opportunity with both hands, but it would mean giving up my place on the MERT team, wouldn't it?'

'I'm afraid so. The department manager is needed here.'

Conflicting emotions were surging through Georgie. On the one hand, what Lizzie was suggesting would mean a safe, steady job, a job without risk—the next logical step on the career ladder. On the other hand, as a member of the MERT team, she was having to face constant challenges every day. Alongside Logan. And now she knew that was what she had been born to do.

'I'm sorry, Lizzie. If I have a choice, it has to be to stay with the MERT team. I hope you understand.'

Lizzie looked at her thoughtfully, a smile playing at the corners of her mouth. 'And a certain Dr Logan Harris has nothing to do with that decision?'

Heat flooded Georgie's cheeks. Damn. She made herself sit up tall and squared her shoulders.

'I have no idea what you're talking about, Lizzie,' she said with as much dignity as possible. 'So, if it's okay with you, I'd like to get back to work.'

But as she walked to the door Lizzie spoke, laughter in her voice. 'No idea what I'm talking about? Just who are you trying to kid? Anyone can see the pair of you are made for each other. Mark my words, Georgie McArthur. Your days of singledom are well and truly marked.'

Georgie didn't deign to answer. Let everyone think what they liked. None of them knew Logan the way she did—and how impossible a future was for them.

Towards the end of the week, Logan sought Georgie out.

'The forecast for Saturday is good. I thought you might like to take another flight with me. I need to keep up my hours and I'd like the company.'

Georgie's pulse quickened. Innocent though the invitation appeared on the surface, the expression in Logan's eyes told her otherwise.

'I don't think that's a good idea,' she said softly. 'Besides, I promised Jess a day in the park on Saturday. There's a fair with a bouncy castle and pony rides and all sorts of other things to delight a three-year-old. So, sorry. No can do.'

'In that case,' Logan replied, with that determined look back in his eye, 'why don't I come too?'

Georgie's heart thudded against her ribs. The last thing she'd expected was for Logan to want to spend time with her and her daughter.

'If you like,' she said casually. 'I can't see that it would be your cup of tea, however.'

Logan grinned at her and her heart beat faster. 'That's just it,' he said, his voice low. 'I don't think you have any idea what my cup of tea is. If the only way I can get you to go out with me is by going to a park, then so be it.' He groaned in mock despair. 'If my mates could hear what I just said, they'd never believe it.'

Georgie laughed. 'Okay, you're on. But I'm warning you, feeding the ducks is obligatory—as is everything else. Except perhaps the bouncy castle. Somehow I think you might be excused from that. I'll bring the picnic.'

The weather remained sunny and bright until Saturday. Jess woke up Georgie by jumping into bed beside her.

'Come on, Mummy. Time to go.'

Georgie squinted at the clock. 6:00 a.m. Early even by Jess's standards. She hid a sigh, knowing there was no chance her daughter would let her sleep.

'Okay, I'm up,' she said, pushing the duvet aside and fumbling for her dressing gown. 'But you need to be quiet. We don't want to wake Gran, do we?'

By the time she was showered and dressed, Jess's excitement had almost reached fever pitch. Her daughter was standing by the door, holding her teddy in one hand and a juice in the other. She had attempted to get dressed herself, but had somehow managed to put her T-shirt on inside out and her shorts back to front. Something deep down in Georgie shifted as she looked at her little girl. She was her world and she would do anything to save her from heartache. In which case, was she being wise allowing Logan into their lives? Despite what everyone said, the more attached Jess—both of them—got to him, the harder it would be when he left.

It was too late to change her mind now. She could hardly phone Logan and tell him not to come—and she knew she didn't want to. She recalled her mother's advice and she was right. She had to stop thinking of what might happen and focus on the here and now. She couldn't hide from life any longer and she couldn't protect her daughter from disappointment and heartache either, no matter how much she might want to.

She re-dressed Jess and made her eat breakfast, and by then her mother was up. While Mary kept Jess occupied, Georgie slipped out to the delicatessen for their picnic. She loaded her basket with sun-ripened tomatoes and the deli's speciality—home-made quiches. She added crusty bread and cheese and some fruit smoothies. When she'd finished, she had enough food to feed an army. The thought made her wince before she pushed it away. She had promised herself she would enjoy the day and that's what she would do.

As she pulled up outside, she saw that Logan's car was already in the driveway. She glanced at her watch. It was just a little after nine. Her shopping had taken her much longer than expected and Logan must have turned up at nine on the dot.

Inside, Jess was hopping from foot to foot while Logan and her mother chatted. Georgie's heart started its familiar rat-a-tat when she saw him. He looked delicious in a T-shirt and black, thigh-hugging jeans. His closely cropped hair had grown in the time he had been in Glasgow and it suited him longer. He had nicked himself shaving and Georgie had to stop herself from leaning across and touching his face.

When Logan saw her, he got to his feet.

'Sorry. I arrived a bit early.' He said. 'Your mother's been entertaining me.'

'No, you're bang on time. It's me that's running late. Don't quite know how as my beloved daughter had me up at six.' She ruffled Jess's hair.

'Can we go now, Mummy?' Jess asked plaintively. 'I've been waiting for ever.'

'I just have to pack the cool bag with our picnic, then I'm ready.'

Georgie was grateful she had something to occupy herself with. She needed to get her heart rate under control. How was she going to manage a day without giving herself away?

Logan stooped and placed the backpack he always carried on the table. 'I brought something too,' he said. He fished around in his bag and brought out a couple of books. They were the same series he had been reading to Jess that first day back in Fort William. Georgie was surprised and touched he had remembered.

'You can look at them in the car,' Logan promised Jess, before pulling out a large box of chocolates. 'And these are for your granny. We can't leave her without anything, can we?'

Georgie's mother accepted the gift. 'My favourites,' she said warmly. She turned to her daughter, 'Darling, it's such perfect weather to do some gardening. I want to get the lobelia planted before it's too late and this afternoon there's an old movie I've always wanted to see but managed to miss every time on the television. It'll be such a treat to finally watch it and—' her eyes sparkled happily '—enjoy these chocolates at the same time.'

Georgie felt a brief pang of guilt. Her mother should be able to put her feet up whenever she wanted to, not just as a special treat. Maybe it was time she seriously pressurised Mary to go back to Fort William and her own life? She and Jess would cope. She decided to discuss it with her mother later that evening.

'Okay,' Logan said. 'Let's get the troops on the move. Quick march to the car.'

The park was reasonably quiet when they arrived and they found a parking spot easily. It would be much busier in an hour or so, Georgie knew from experience.

Jess was in a frenzy as she tried to decide what to do first. In the end she decided on the bouncy castle, telling Logan and Georgie firmly that they had to watch her as she bounced.

Georgie slid a look in Logan's direction.

'I hope you aren't going to be bored out of your mind,' she said. 'This must be as far away from your usual life as it's possible to get.'

Logan looked into the distance, his eyes hooded. Then he smiled.

'You could say that. But it's great. Makes me realise what I've been missing.'

The expression in his eyes caused Georgie's heart to falter. What was he suggesting? Could he possibly mean that he was getting tired of his nomadic existence in the army?

Before he could say anything else, Jess was off the bouncy castle and had grabbed Georgie and Logan by the hand.

'I want to go on a ride now,' she said. 'I want to go on the train and I want to go on the horses and I want to go on the big wheel and the boat on the lake. After that I want—'

'Hold on.' Georgie laughed. 'One thing at a time. Why don't we go on the boat, then you can go on the carousel? After that we can have our picnic lunch and do some of the other rides. Okay?'

There was no queue as yet for the boats so they were able to get out on the lake quickly. Logan picked up the oars and began to row.

'Hey,' Georgie protested. 'How do you know I didn't want to row?'

Logan looked at her in surprise. 'Do you?' he said.

'No, not really. I just want you to know I could, if I wanted to.'

Logan's eyes travelled the length of her body. Georgie was convinced that the temperature had risen a couple of degrees in the last ten seconds, and she knew he was also remembering their day on the island.

'I'm sure you could,' he drawled, looking unconvinced.

'I'll have you know I've been at the gym four times in the

last week,' Georgie said defensively. Then, catching the laughter in his brown eyes, she flushed. 'Okay, maybe three times, but I am getting fitter. Another few months and I'll be back to the same weight and level of fitness I was before Jess was born.'

'I like you just the way you are,' Logan responded lazily. 'Far too many women think being stick thin is the only way to be. I prefer a few curves myself.' This time Georgie knew it wasn't the heat of the sun that was making her temperature rise. The look in his eyes told her that he too was thinking of their love-making and the way he had explored every inch of her with his eyes then his lips. A delicious shiver coursed through her body.

'Don't you think your mummy is perfect the way she is, Jess?' he asked.

Jess, who had been listening to the adults, confusion written all over her face, giggled. 'I think she's the beautifulest mummy in the whole wide world.'

Logan's grin grew wider. 'And I agree with you,' he said.

After their boat trip, they watched in companionable silence as Jess rode on the carousel. Logan showed no sign of impatience or boredom despite Jess insisting on staying on for several goes.

Eventually, Georgie managed to extract her daughter from the ride. The park was beginning to fill up as people continued to pour in.

'Let's find a spot for our picnic before the best are all taken,' Georgie suggested.

They found a place in the shade under an oak tree, a reasonable distance from the rest of the picnickers.

Georgie spread the thick tartan rug she had brought from home on the ground and tossed a few cushions on it. A short distance away, a miniature train was making its way round a track, towing several carriages with children.

'Can Uncle Logan take me on the train before we have our picnic, Mummy?'

'I'm not sure he'll fit on that train.' Georgie laughed. 'He's a bit big.'

'There's other daddies on the train,' Jess persisted. 'Look!' She pointed her finger, and, sure enough, several fathers as well as mothers were perched on the train, holding their children. But Georgie wasn't really looking. Her daughter's words were ringing in her ears. *The other daddies.* Oh, no. Her worst fears were being realised. Jess had latched onto Logan and had clearly decided that Logan was the nearest thing to a daddy she had. Georgie slid a horrified glance at Logan. Sure enough, he looked dismayed. All this was probably more than he had bargained for when he had agreed to the day out. Georgie wondered if, after today, he would be in full retreat. Well, there was nothing she could do about it. She and Jess were a package and she had never pretended otherwise.

Logan recovered quickly. 'Sure, I'll go with you,' he said. Jess squealed with delight and Logan took her by the waist and swung her onto his shoulders. Georgie's heart stumbled as she watched them move towards the train. Anyone watching would assume they were father and daughter.

As she unpacked their picnic she continued to watch them with half an eye. She saw them get on the train, Logan placing Jess carefully in front and then climbing on behind her. She had to laugh. His legs were so long that bent they were practically up to his ears. He looked as awkward as she had ever seen him and when the child-sized train puffed its way past her, he raised his hand in a wave and smiled wryly. Jess had no such qualms. She yelled and waved vigorously at her mother, clearly having the time of her life.

Georgie had their picnic laid out, the bread buttered and the salad tossed, when Jess and Logan returned.

'You should have come too, Mummy. It was so much fun. You liked it too, didn't you, Uncle Logan?'

'Sure did, honey. I wouldn't have missed it for the world.' His smile was wide. 'But next time's Mummy's turn.'

As they ate, Jess chattered non-stop. 'I'm having so-o-o much fun. I wish we could do this every day.'

'Me too,' Logan said quietly. This time his eyes were serious. Georgie's world tilted as he held her gaze. She knew she had been kidding herself. She didn't want a short-term relationship with this man. She loved him. Heart and soul. Whatever fears she still had and whatever the future held in store, she knew that she would rather face it all than a life without this man.

By the time they left the park, Jess was flagging. She had done so much running around she had exhausted herself. Logan picked her up and she buried her face in his neck and promptly fell asleep.

She was still dead to the world when they reached Georgie's house. Logan carried the sleeping child inside.

'Where do you want her?' he asked softly.

'I think I'll just put her to bed. She was up so early, she'll be out for the count until morning.'

She led the way to Jess's bedroom, peeling back the pink duvet so that Logan could lay her down. She quickly removed her daughter's outer clothes, covered her up and tiptoed out of the room.

Georgie peeped into the sitting room. Her mother was dozing in front of the television, the open box of chocolates by her arm.

Silently, she slipped into the kitchen. Logan was leaning against the counter. He reached out and pulled her against him. She revelled in the feel of his hard body against the length of hers, and warmth spread from her lower abdomen.

Logan brushed a hand along her jaw down to her neck. Shivers of desire coursed through her body.

'Come home with me,' he whispered into her ear.

'I can't,' she pleaded softly, turning her face up to his. His lips came down on hers and he kissed her hungrily as if it were the first and last time.

'I've been thinking about making love to you all day.' He groaned against her mouth.

A sound from the sitting room alerted Georgie and she jerked away from Logan, hoping desperately her flushed cheeks wouldn't betray her.

Her mother came into the kitchen, blinking sleepily.

'I didn't hear you come in.' She yawned. 'You should have woken me.'

'We haven't been back very long.' Georgie struggled to keep her voice steady. 'Anyway, you looked so peaceful, Mum, I couldn't bear to wake you.'

'Where's Jess?'

'She's in bed. Absolutely exhausted. I think that will be her until morning.'

'In which case, what are you two still doing here? Away the pair of you go and have some fun while you can.'

Georgie felt her face grow even redder, if that were possible. 'I don't think…'

Logan grinned wolfishly, before flashing a smile at her mother.

'I was just trying to persuade your daughter to do just that. Are you sure you don't mind babysitting?'

'Goodness, no. Jess is in bed and I've had the whole day relaxing. You two youngsters should make the most of the opportunity to have some adult time.'

Georgie hid a smile at her mother's choice of words. Until today when she had seen him on the train, she couldn't have imagined anyone thinking of him as a youngster. She bent and kissed her mother's cheek.

'I'm not going anywhere until I have had a shower and a change of clothing,' she said firmly. 'So if I can trust you not to bring out the baby albums, Mum, at least not of me, I'll leave you two for twenty minutes.'

'Baby photos. Now, there's a thought,' Logan said. 'Any chance of a peek, Mary, while we're waiting?'

Knowing that there was little she could do about it, Georgie left them alone. She showered quickly, every nerve cell in her body tingling with anticipation. She doubted they would be getting to dinner any time soon.

Selecting her favourite undies and a summer dress, she slicked on some lipstick and mascara. Her cheeks were already bright with colour so there was no need for any blusher.

When she returned to the kitchen, she was relieved to find the baby albums weren't out. Instead, Logan and her mother seemed to be engaged in a serious discussion. Hearing her approach, Logan stopped in mid-sentence and let out a low whistle of approval.

There was no doubt in Georgie's mind that her mother had been quizzing him thoroughly about his private life. Logan would be no match for her highly developed interrogation skills. The sooner she got him out of there, the better.

Logan got to his feet. 'Dinner?' he said mildly.

Georgie's stomach was churning so much she couldn't imagine being able to chew a mouthful. She nodded mutely.

When they got into the car, Logan looked at her.

'You are so very beautiful,' he said, pulling her towards him and kissing her gently on the lips. 'I don't know about you, but I don't think I could eat a thing—not at the moment anyway.' From the hungry look in his eyes there was no mistaking his intent and Georgie couldn't bring herself to play games. The truth was, all she had been thinking of the whole day was being in his arms again.

Logan's flat was in a new development overlooking the Clyde and his flat on the tenth floor had impressive views of the river.

It was sparsely furnished and Georgie formed the distinct impression he hardly used it. There were a few books lying on the coffee table—an autobiography by the American president and biographies of Churchill and Napoleon amongst others. In one corner, a steel string guitar was propped against the wall. There was also a state-of–the-art music system, the speakers dominating the room. Apart from these items, there were no personal effects. No photos, no little knick-knacks, no soft furnishings. It was the flat of a man who used it to eat and sleep in. It was not a home.

But she only had time for the briefest inspection before she was in Logan's arms. He kissed her hungrily and she responded, hooking her legs around his hips. He cradled her bottom in his hands and, still kissing, he carried her towards his bedroom and laid her gently on the bed. Then they were pulling at each other's clothes, touching each other, as if the world was about to come to an end.

Much later, as Georgie, wrapped in a sheet, stood looking out at early evening sunshine glistening on the river below, Logan came to stand behind her, enfolding her in his arms. She leaned against him, revelling in the feeling of security and contentment.

'Why don't you have a permanent home?' she asked. 'Somewhere to go when you're not overseas with the army?'

'I've never seen the point. I prefer to visit a different city or country when I have time off, either competing or just touring. There is so much of the world to see, and so little time to see it.'

'Don't you miss not having one place to come back to?' She swivelled round in his arms so she could read his expression.

'I can't say I do. In fact, I can think of nothing worse than being stuck in the same spot. I think it would drive me mad eventually.'

Georgie's heart sank. What else did she expect? She had walked into this with her eyes wide open, but that had been before she had fallen in love with him. All this was great, lovely. Now she was greedy and she wanted more. When he left, as he inevitably would, her heart was going to be shattered.

'Tell me about your parents,' she said softly. 'What were they like? Why don't you talk about them?'

He stiffened and the now familiar, guarded look returned to his eyes. He moved away and fiddled around with his music system. The sounds of Rachmaninov filled the air.

'Logan?' she persisted.

He refused to meet her gaze. 'I don't know about you, but I'm starving. Shall we send out for something?' he said, ignoring her question.

Only moments before she could have sworn food was the last thing on his mind. Something had changed, the atmosphere had cooled. Now she felt as if she'd been slapped and all her misgivings come rushing back. He seemed determined not to let her get too close to him.

'Why don't we go out?' Georgie said. 'It's a beautiful evening.' Off balance at the coolness that seemed to have descended between them, she wanted to put some distance between them, even if for a short while. She couldn't think clearly when he was so close.

'Sure. Anything you like. There's a little place on the river that serves meals until late. Atmosphere's great and the food's not bad either. I go there most evenings. Can't say cooking is my thing.'

They dressed quickly, without speaking, and stepped out into the evening air. Thoughts were whirling around Georgie's head. What was she doing? It was madness spending time with a man who was going to break her heart. A man who wouldn't open up to her, either because he didn't trust her or because he didn't see a future for them. Why hadn't she got out of the relationship when she still could? But she knew the answer. Because she was tired of licking her wounds and hiding from life. If nothing else, Logan had made her feel alive again, and if that hurt, at least it was better than feeling nothing. Or so she had thought. Now she wasn't so sure.

The back lane Logan took as a shortcut was quiet, apart from three youths at the other end. Ahead of them they became aware of a scuffle. It looked as if the young men were harassing an elderly man on his own. Georgie sensed a change in Logan. There was a watchfulness, an intense stillness about him as he kept his eyes pinned on them. He pulled her closer to his side as they continued to walk towards the group.

Suddenly one of the trio viciously punched the older man in the stomach. He gripped his middle in disbelief, before sinking to his knees.

'Hey. Leave him alone!' Logan shouted, and started sprinting towards them. Rooted to the spot, Georgie could only stand and watch. Thankfully when they saw Logan's six feet three of solid muscle heading towards them the youths turned tail and ran.

Logan looked after them as if considering whether to give chase, but then he dropped to his knees beside the fallen man, feeling for a pulse.

'Is he all right?' Georgie asked as she ran up to them.

Logan ripped open the fallen man's shirt and examined the wound. 'He's been stabbed. Phone 999 and get the police and ambulance here. Tell them to hurry.'

Georgie drew in a sharp breath when she saw the extent of the injury but carried on dialling. The man had been stabbed in his chest and Georgie knew from experience that they had to get the victim to hospital as a matter of urgency. Treating a knife wound was notoriously difficult and fraught with complications as often the worst damage was hidden below the surface.

She gave their location to the ambulance controller and a brief description of the injury. When she disconnected, Logan had finished examining the fallen man and was looking worried.

'He's got a tension pneumothorax,' he said tightly, whipping off his jacket to cover the man. 'I'm going to have to do something, and quick. We can't wait for the ambulance.'

Georgie's heart kicked against her ribs. Although they had practised for this type of scenario, she had never imagined they would have to do it. Alone. In the street. And with what?

'I'm going to fetch my bag from the flat,' Logan said. 'I need you to stay with him while I go and get it. Concentrate on keeping him breathing. Can you do that?'

Don't leave me here, Georgie wanted to shout. But she realised Logan was right. He would be much faster than her getting back to his apartment and he knew where the bag was. She nodded. And then Logan was running.

Minutes ticked by slowly. Where the hell was the ambulance? She checked her patient's breathing. It was shallow and rapid and he was becoming cyanosed. He could die at any time unless something was done to help him breathe.

'Not while I have anything to do with it,' she muttered, knowing no one could hear her. The back lane was quiet and remained deserted. Georgie could hear the swish of tyres on tarmac a few metres away, but it might have been hundreds of metres for all the use it could do them.

She staunched the bleeding chest wound with one hand while she kept her fingers on his carotid pulse and her eyes on his chest. If he arrested, she would have to perform CPR long enough for the ambulance to arrive or Logan to return. It was what the last weeks of training had been all about. Keeping the patient alive long enough to get them to hospital.

Just as she thought she could no longer feel a pulse, Logan returned. As she raised her eyes from the victim she heard the siren of an ambulance speeding towards them. Logan must have heard it, but took no notice. Taking a large-size IV cannula, he plunged it into the man's chest close to the stab wound but away from the heart. There was an immediate whoosh of air as the tense air pocket was released. Almost miraculously Georgie felt the result.

'He's got a pulse,' she said, hugely relieved.

'Quick, help me get an IV line in as well just in case he's haemorrhaging,' responded Logan, totally focused on the elderly man.

Georgie efficiently inserted the IV line as the paramedics rushed to their side. Georgie updated them, outlining what she and Logan had done so far.

Logan stood while the paramedics hustled the injured man onto a stretcher and into the ambulance.

'Go home, Georgie. Call a taxi for yourself. I'll have to go with him to hospital. And I need you to be safe.' He paused for a moment, cupping her chin in his hand. 'Are you okay?'

Georgie nodded. But she wasn't sure if she was. For a

moment back there she'd thought Logan was going to run after the youths and her heart had stopped.

It was all more than she could bear.

The taxi driver looked at her strangely when he noted her blood-splattered clothes, but she didn't have the energy to explain. Now it was all over, she felt washed out. Her hands were shaking. She leaned back in her seat. They had probably saved a man's life. If it hadn't been for them, the victim might not have been discovered until it was too late. A thrill ran though her. She got what attracted Logan to this kind of emergency medicine. It wouldn't be for everyone. Too high-pressure for a start, but Georgie knew that in this way at least she was similar to Logan.

Then the memory of him facing up to the thugs came rushing back and with it a gut-wrenching nausea. They could so easily have turned on him and stabbed him too. Hadn't he known that? But she knew with absolute certainty that even if he had, it wouldn't have stopped him. Logan was the kind of man who would never let fear prevent him from doing what he thought was right. And if he lost his own life in the process? He would consider it part of the job. She shivered. Why had he come into her life? Why did it have to be him of all people she had fallen in love with? As she paid the driver and climbed out of the cab, she made up her mind. There was no future for her in this re-lationship. She just wasn't up to it. She had to end it before she got in any deeper. The thought broke her heart all over again.

Logan phoned a couple of hours later to say that the man had been taken to ITU and was holding his own. The police had taken a statement from him and wanted to speak to her too, but he had persuaded them to wait until the morning.

'You did great,' he said approvingly.

'I was scared witless.'

He laughed. 'But you didn't let your fear get in the way.'
Little did he know that she was going to do exactly that. 'I'm
sorry the evening didn't turn out the way we planned. What
about tomorrow night?'

'I'm sorry. I can't.'

'Monday night, then?'

'No. Look, Logan, we need to talk.'

There was a long silence on the other end of the phone.
'Does that mean what it usually does?' He sounded perplexed.
As well he might be. After all, only hours earlier she had been
in his bed and in his arms.

'Can we talk about it later?'

'Let's talk about it now,' he said firmly. 'I'm on my way over.'

Before she could protest, he disconnected. Her heart beating
uncomfortably, she put on some clothes and went to wait for
him in the sitting room. When she heard his car pull up she
slipped outside, not wanting to take the chance her mother
would wake up and hear her.

'Okay.' He looked at her, his mouth set in a grim line. 'Talk
to me.'

'I can't do this,' she said. 'I'm sorry, I thought I could but I
can't. You could have been killed back there. You could be
killed any time and I'm done with losing people I…' Just in time
she stopped herself from saying 'love'. 'People I care about.'

'Agreed. We could *all* die at any time. Working in emergency
medicine, you must know that. People get hurt driving their
cars, walking their kids to school, in a million different ways.
We hope it won't happen to us and mostly it doesn't.'

'It's different for you. Your job takes you into danger all
the time.'

He laughed but there was no mirth in the sound. 'I don't

know what you think I do, but when I'm on a tour, most of the time I'm working at the field hospital. It's safe. Or as safe as almost anywhere in these times.'

'Most of the time?' she repeated.

'Sometimes I accompany the men out on patrol,' he admitted. 'I'm a full-time army medic. It's my job.'

'That's what I mean. You can't tell me that there's not a huge risk you'll be killed. A much greater risk than for most people.'

'Not huge.' He drew a line down her jaw with one long finger. She resented the way her body reacted to his slightest touch. When he did that she couldn't think clearly. When he touched her all she could think of was the here and now, not the future. But she had to think about the future. Even if she didn't owe it to herself, she owed it to Jess.

She traced the scar on his face with a finger. 'How *did* you get this?' she said softly.

Logan was quiet for a while. 'I was out on patrol with the platoon one day. We doctors take it in turn to go out with the men behind the front line, so when the shooting starts we're right there.'

Georgie glanced up at him. His eyes were dark, unfathomable pools.

'We were ambushed. Outside a village. There were several casualties. One of the injured men had fallen in the open. He was bleeding badly.' His voice was quiet, almost matter-of-fact, but Georgie could hear the anguish behind his words.

'I knew if we couldn't get to him, he'd bleed to death. So three of the other soldiers and I made a dash for him. We managed to get him to safety, but not before…' He rubbed his scar ruefully. 'Not before I caught a bullet. Luckily, it only grazed me.' He smiled. 'Spoiled my looks, but that's it.'

'And the other soldiers? The injured man? Did they make it?'

'Thankfully, yes. We were lucky that time. A Chinook was able to evacuate us all a short time later.'

Georgie guessed there was more to the story than Logan was telling her, but she didn't press him. She wasn't at all surprised he had risked his life—hadn't everything she'd learned about this man told her that he would do so without the slightest hesitation? Although she hated the thought, his actions were what made him the man he was. And that was the trouble. She couldn't see a future with that kind of man. No matter how much she wanted to.

Logan grasped her by the shoulders. 'I think I'm in love with you. Damn it, I know I'm in love with you and it scares me to death. I didn't think I would ever say those words. I love you, Georgie McArthur and I want you to be my wife.' His voice was ragged.

Happiness blossomed as she heard the words. He loved her. But then her heart chilled. It was no use. She couldn't say yes to a life that would destroy her and consequently him too.

'I plan to live a long, long life and I want you in it. I want to grow old with you, have babies with you. The whole shooting match. Do you understand what I'm saying? I want us to spend the rest of our lives together.'

She shook her head, hating the fact she was about to hurt him. She had to ask—even if she strongly suspected she knew the answer.

'Will you give up the army? Take a permanent job in a civilian hospital somewhere? It doesn't have to be here. Any-where in the world and I would go with you. Even if it means leaving my family. With your experience, you'd get a job wherever you wanted.'

The pain and regret in his eyes almost crushed her.

'The army is my life, Georgie. It's what I know. Who I am. Please don't ask me to give it up.'

She reached out her hand and touched him gently on the face. 'Then it's no use. Can't you see? I couldn't live like that. Waiting in fear for a call that could come any time to tell me you're dead. It would eat away at me and I would try and change you. Try and turn you from the man I love into someone else. You'd start to hate me for it.'

'But you do love me?'

'Yes.' Her voice was small. Too much to ask him to change.

'Then take a chance. Isn't it better to risk everything than not live at all?'

'I wish I were different. But I'm not. Can't we just carry on the way we are? Be friends? Make the most of the time we have together before you have to go away again?'

This time it was Logan who shook his head. 'Don't you know by now that I'm an all-or-nothing man? Right now I want all of you. If you truly loved me, you would take a chance on us.' As she made to protest, he stopped her words, laying a finger on her lips. 'I thought you were braver than this, Georgie. I can see I was mistaken. The woman I want to spend the rest of my life with has to accept me the way I am. I can't be any other way. You're right. If I were forced to stop what I love doing, it would eat me up inside. Eventually it would kill the love between us as surely as any bullet.'

'Then there's nothing left to be said,' she replied sadly. She turned to go back into the house, knowing that tears weren't far away. If she broke down now, and he pulled her into his arms, she would never be able to let him go. And she loved him too much not to.

Logan returned to his flat. His bed was still rumpled where they had made love and Georgie's perfume lingered everywhere. He surveyed his flat with a critical eye, seeing it through Georgie's eyes. She was right. It was as impersonal as a hotel room. Living like this had never bothered him—until now. Georgie had given him a taste of what life could be like. A life where he had a family to come home to.

He crossed over to the window and gazed out onto the river. Shouldn't he do what she asked? She was right about one thing. He could easily find a job in a civilian hospital, possibly even at the Glasgow City General; the powers that be had made it clear that they were happy with the way the service was going and had already earmarked funds to keep it going as a permanent service. Wouldn't it be worth it to have what she was offering?

But leave the army? The men who needed him? However much he loved Georgie, couldn't she see it wasn't fair to ask that of him? The thing was, he wanted the woman he loved to love him back. Unconditionally. Without strings. No matter how tough life got. Someone who wouldn't give up when the going got rough. Someone the complete opposite from his mother. He'd thought he'd found that woman in Georgie. And he'd been wrong. He should have listened to his gut instinct and kept well away from her when he'd had the chance. If he had, he would never have known how much he wanted the life he saw dangling tantalisingly in front of him. But she didn't love him enough. It was time he accepted that.

CHAPTER TEN

THE next couple of weeks were painful for Georgie. Every time she saw Logan she would catch her breath. True to his word, he kept his distance. Oh, he was just as polite and friendly as always, but he didn't ask her out again and he never indicated with a word or look that she meant anything to him. Even that they had been lovers. What else did she expect? She had told him there was no future for them. Not the way things were. And he had made it perfectly clear he couldn't—wouldn't—take anything less than her total acceptance of him and his life. And if her heart was breaking into tiny pieces, it was better that it happened now. Time would heal. Hadn't she already learned that?

Whatever. It was better this way. She would get over him. He would move on and she would return to her predictable, happy, safe life.

No one seemed to notice the tension between them, which was a relief. The rescue service was going through a quiet spell. Georgie had gone out with Nick to a car accident, which had happily turned out to be less serious than had been reported. Sally and Nick had attended a rider who had fallen and had suspected head injuries, and Sally was clearly relishing her new role.

'The rider's doing well,' she confided in Georgie. 'If we

hadn't been there, if Nick hadn't been able to keep her breathing till we got her to hospital, it might have been a different story.'

This was exactly the kind of emergency they had been trained to deal with and the new rescue service was already making an impact.

So much of an impact that other A and E departments were beginning to take notice. If theirs continued to do well, the Scottish executive that dealt with the funding of these extra national services had agreed to look at setting up similar services in Edinburgh and Aberdeen. In fact, Logan had been away for a week visiting the other units and had only returned that morning.

This time it was Lata who told them about the call. 'Ambulance Control has just phoned in. There is a report of a multiple pileup on the A82 going towards Lochgilphead. They want to know if you want the 'copter to pick you up. I assumed you do.'

Logan smiled. 'You bet. What about you, Georgie? The helicopter can only take two of us. Nick and Lata would be better staying here to receive any casualties.'

Mouth suddenly dry, Georgie could only nod. It would be the first time they'd be alone together since the night at her house and she wondered if he'd say anything. Like what? I'm going to give up the army to be with you? He'd already made it clear that wasn't going to happen.

'Lata, how soon until the helicopter's here?' Logan asked.

'They're already on their way. They'll be on the helipad in three minutes.'

Before Georgie realised it, she was fully suited and on her way to the helipad. The RAF helicopter had already touched down and was waiting with its rotors still whirling.

'Copy what I do.' Logan yelled to make himself heard above the noise. 'But whatever you do, keep your head down.'

Georgie mimicked his crouching run, following close behind him. He jumped into the helicopter and pulled her in unceremoniously beside him. As the helicopter took off, Georgie fell against Logan. For the briefest of moments he held her in his arms, tightly against his chest. Then, as soon as the helicopter straightened out he let her go.

The paramedic in the back held out headsets for both of them. Logan fastened one to his helmet and, taking Georgie's, placed it securely on her head. As his fingers brushed her cheeks she felt a tingle zip through her right to her toes.

Her heart started beating wildly, and she tried to tell herself it was the usual adrenaline rush that accompanied emergencies.

'There are three cars involved, as far as we know,' a disembodied voice came through her earphones into her ears. 'The fire service and one ambulance are already at the scene. Another is on its way from Glasgow, but I think we'll get there long before it does.'

'Roger that. What do we know about the condition of the casualties?'

'Not too much. The driver of one of the cars is trapped at the moment, and the fire crew are attempting to cut him free. His status hasn't been confirmed yet. There are at least four other casualties, including a child, but their condition is not yet known.'

By the time they arrived at the scene, the firemen and police had the road cordoned off and the helicopter was able to land nearby on the road.

'We're on.' Logan grinned at her. 'Stay close to me.'

They ran the few metres to the accident scene. Georgie sucked in a breath. Two of the cars were embedded in each other, the third a short distance away, its front wheels perilously close to a steep drop. The car that the fire service was working on looked so badly damaged it was difficult for Georgie to believe anyone could have survived.

The senior fire officer on the scene detached himself from his crew and strode towards Georgie and Logan, his expression grim.

'We have one driver trapped by his legs. We're going to have to cut him out. We're worried that once we do, we might be left to deal with an uncontrollable bleed. He's been drifting in and out of consciousness since we arrived.' He pointed to the car near the cliff face. 'There's a mother and child in there. The mother is conscious, but can't move. Not until we secure the car. The other car's occupant has only minor injuries. But until we know what caused the accident we should keep an eye on him.'

The sound of heavy cutters filled the air, making it difficult to hear.

'Where to first?' Georgie asked Logan.

'I'll take the trapped man. You check out the mother and child.' Logan was taking his backpack off his shoulders. 'But I don't want you to do anything that might put yourself in danger. Do you understand? You're not to go in that car until the firemen have made it stable. Do you hear me?'

Yeah, right. Of course she was going to do nothing.

Logan moved towards his patient. Georgie ran to the car with the mother and child. She winced when she saw the car and its precarious position. The car had come to rest with its front wheels hanging over the edge of the cliff. The slightest movement could topple it over at any time. And if it went… She shuddered. There was no way the passengers inside would survive.

The firefighters were securing a heavy rope around the rear axle. Georgie tiptoed as close to the car as she could get and peered through the window. In the rear a baby was strapped into a car seat and he, or she, was crying furiously. Despite the obvious distress, that was a good sign. Had the baby been quiet,

Georgie would have been more worried. In the front, in the driver's seat, was the mother. Georgie could just make out the back of her head.

'Can you hear me?' she shouted.

The woman tried to turn her head in the direction of Georgie's voice.

'No, don't move a muscle,' Georgie shouted, alarmed. 'We'll get to you in a sec. Your baby seems fine and the fire engine is going to pull your car to safety. What's your name?'

'Lucy,' the woman gasped. 'Please get my baby out of the car.'

'Everything's going to be all right, Lucy. Everyone is doing everything they can. Just be patient. We'll soon have you out of there.'

Georgie whirled around. What was taking so long? If the fire crew didn't get a move on, the woman might panic and reach for her child. Any movement could send the car over the edge or, if the woman had a spinal injury, lead to paralysis.

Just then there was a crunch of metal on rock and the car slipped forward. The mother screamed. Georgie closed her eyes, unable to bring herself to look. A second later she forced them open again. Thankfully the cable the firemen had attached to the car had stopped the vehicle from slipping more than a few metres down the mountainside. The fire engine was bearing the weight, preventing its further descent. The baby was screaming in earnest now.

'Leave it to us, nurse. We've got it. You need to move out of the way while we pull it up.' A fireman appeared at her side and, taking her gently by the elbow, attempted to move her out of the way.

'Step back?' Georgie replied. 'Not on your life. The woman could have a spinal injury. She needs to be immobilised before we can risk moving the car.' She glanced around frantically for

Logan but he was preoccupied with his patient. 'Does anyone have a rope?'

'There's one in the fire engine,' one of the men told her. 'But there's no way we're going to let you go down there. One of us will go.'

'For God's sake, I can do this. We don't have time to argue. Get me the rope and lower me down. I'll get a neck brace on then you can pull the car up.'

The firefighter wasn't convinced. 'Look, miss, if that car slips at all, it could crush you.'

'Or you,' Georgie responded calmly. 'But I'm a trained climber and a medic. Can you say that? Now, please, we're wasting time.'

Resigned, the fireman tied the rope one of the others had fetched from the engine and tied it firmly around Georgie's waist. Before he could protest further, Georgie had slipped over the side and was carefully picking her way down the slope.

When she got to the car, the baby's cries had stopped in response to the mother's voice. Wide, frightened eyes found hers.

'It's okay,' Georgie said, forcing a smile. 'I'm just going to reach through your window and fix this collar round your neck. Then we'll pull you and the car up. How does that sound?'

She got a weak smile in response. 'Seeing as I'm not really in a position to get myself out of here, I guess I'll just have to do what I'm told. But could you make it quick, please?'

As rapidly as she could, Georgie retrieved the neck brace from her backpack and reaching into the car carefully, without adding any weight, fixed the collar and stabilised the woman's neck.

'The neck brace will help, but try and keep as still as you can until the car is up. Okay? I'll see you up there.' And with a final smile Georgie left her and scrambled back up to the top.

There was nothing more Georgie could do until the firemen had pulled the car to safety. It would take them time, she knew. They would want to take it slowly so as not to cause any more damage to the woman's neck. 'Call me the minute it's up,' she yelled, and ran across to the driver of the third vehicle. The ambulance crew had checked him out and he was sitting in the back of the ambulance, an oxygen mask covering his face.

'He was looking a little cyanosed and his sats were low so we put him on oxygen as a precaution,' the paramedic told Georgie. 'He can't remember much about what happened, so we can't be sure that he didn't lose consciousness and cause the accident. We're just waiting for the doctor to have a quick look before we get on our way.'

Logan was inside the other car, alongside the driver. The roof had been completely removed and with the help of one of the paramedics Logan was fitting a neck brace to the occupant.

Georgie sprinted across. 'Do you need help?' she asked.

Logan glanced up. 'Not right now. The fire crew are going to cut away the part of the car that is trapping his legs. I might need you then. How are the other casualties?'

'The car with the mother and baby is being pulled up now. I haven't been able to examine them properly, but the baby is crying and the mother is conscious. I've fitted a neck brace on the mother.' Logan's mouth tightened as he realised what she must have done. She went on before he had a chance to say anything. 'Neither seems to be badly injured, although we'll need to check them out to be sure. The driver of the other car is being given oxygen by the paramedics. I think they suspect a heart attack. Should they take him to hospital or will we take him in the helicopter?'

'It could take us another thirty minutes before we get this driver out. The nearest hospital is in Oban. What's that? About thirty minutes away?' Logan paused. 'Ask one of the paramedics to go with him in the helicopter. And ask the helicopter crew to return as soon as they can.'

'What about the woman and her baby? What if they need immediate evacuation?'

Logan looked her in the eye. 'We work with what we know. Just do as I say. Any time spent arguing is time wasted. I'll check on the mother and baby as soon as I can.' His eyes were calm, his voice firm. Georgie knew it would be pointless to argue. He was right—wasting time would help no one and he was the one with this kind of experience. 'You need to be my eyes and ears. Trust your instinct.'

She sped back to the ambulance and repeated to the paramedics what Logan had told her. The driver with the suspected heart-attack still didn't look good.

'His blood pressure's dropping,' the paramedic said quietly. Georgie could hear the concern in her voice.

'Okay, let's get him loaded onto the helicopter. One of you has to go with him. I have to stay here to attend to the woman and child as soon as the car is secure.'

Within minutes the man was securely in the helicopter. The paramedic had placed leads from a portable defibrillator on his chest and from the readout Georgie knew they were dealing with a heart attack. He needed to get to a coronary care unit, and fast.

Minutes later the helicopter took off.

Georgie took a few seconds to get her breathing under control. The woman and her car were still being inched to safety. The trapped man was the current priority. It was possible that the part of the car that was pinning his legs was also acting as a tourniquet. If it was, there was a very real danger that once the pressure was removed, he'd haemorrhage. Georgie knew that he could lose more blood in a very short space of time than they could replace. She was sure that Logan would know what to do. He had told the team it was the type of injury that, unfortunately, he'd had to deal with many times before.

'Georgie, I need you over here,' Logan called.

When she reached him, Logan drew her to the side away from the car.

'The fire crew have reached the point where they're ready to free Alan's legs from the steering column. But one or both of his legs are fractured and we're going to have to sedate him to do that. It's going to be risky, because we haven't secured his airway and he may well stop breathing with the sedation. While you were away I put in a couple of IV lines and got the drugs ready. Can you get ready to give the propofol while I stand by with the laryngeal mask airway? I've explained to Alan what we're going to do, and why.'

The chief fireman signalled they were ready to move the car and at Logan's nod Georgie injected the IV sedation slowly.

'Alan, you'll feel yourself drifting off to sleep as I give you this. The next thing you'll know you'll be in hospital.'

Alan grabbed her hand. 'If I don't make it, tell my wife I love her, please.'

'We're not going to let anything happen to you, Alan,' Georgie soothed, praying she was telling the truth.

Alan wasn't finished. 'We had…argument…morning.' He was struggling to speak. 'Didn't say goodbye.'

Tears burned behind Georgie's eyelids. She knew what it was like not to be able to say goodbye.

As the sedation took effect, Logan supported Alan's head and carefully but precisely passed the tube down his throat. At his nod, Georgie inflated the cuff that would prevent air leaks and squeezed the bag a few times. Logan nodded in the direction of the waiting firefighters. In a few seconds their equipment had pulled the wrecked vehicles a few inches apart.

Then a swarm of helping hands descended and quickly removed Alan from the vehicle and onto a stretcher. To everyone's immense relief the bleeding from Alan's legs wasn't as bad as they had feared. They splinted his legs and very soon they had him in the helicopter, which had returned from Oban and was waiting to take them and their injured patient back to Glasgow.

Logan jumped in beside Alan, and Georgie turned her attention back to the woman and child. While they had been working on Alan, the fire service had got the car up safely and the paramedics had made their assessment of mother and baby.

'All observations, normal. I don't think there is any real cause for concern,' the medic told Georgie. 'We'll pop them in the ambulance and take them to Oban if you want to get going.'

Throughout the journey they kept Alan sedated and monitored his respirations. The noise of the aircraft kept talking to the minimum, but Georgie found she and Logan worked together instinctively, without the need for discussion.

When they got back to the hospital, several staff were waiting to take over.

As the adrenaline seeped away, Georgie felt her knees turn to rubber.

She stumbled into the staffroom and collapsed on the nearest chair. Suddenly a heady sense of exhilaration flooded her body. She'd done it! She had participated in a rescue which had no doubt saved lives, and it felt wonderful. Almost more wonderful was the feeling that she hadn't felt any fear, not even for a second. She had proved to herself she was able to deal with any eventuality the rescue service could throw at her.

She looked up as Logan entered the room, and grinned at him.

'We did great, didn't we?'

Instead of grinning back, he frowned. 'You did well. You were extremely brave. No. Actually, you were reckless. The first rule is that no one puts themselves in danger. We are there to save lives, not to have to carry out a rescue of one of the team. You went against agreed protocols. The first priority is staff safety. The fire crew were there and it is their job to make the scene safe so we can treat the patients. It is not our job to argue with them and do our own thing.' He held up his hands as she started to protest. 'Yes, I know the outcome was good, but it could so easily have gone the other way.'

All the exhilaration rushed out of her, leaving her feeling like a deflated balloon.

'C'mon, Logan. You know I couldn't do *nothing*. If that was your wife and child back there, wouldn't you have wanted someone to go out on a limb for them?'

'But it wasn't my wife and child. We can't make these things personal, Georgie. The moment we do, our judgement goes out the window. You put everyone's life at risk—not just yours.'

The anger in his eyes was unmistakable. It was ironic that he was lecturing her about taking risks.

'You're a fine person to talk,' she responded hotly. 'You're the biggest risk taker of us all.'

'The risks I take are managed, Georgie. Or unavoidable. You didn't have to do what you did. If I thought someone needed to go down to the occupants of the car, I would have gone.'

'But you couldn't go, could you? You had your own situation to deal with. What sort of team member would I be, if I waited for your permission before I did anything? I'd be worse than useless.'

'It's one of the toughest parts of the job. Who to deal with first.' For a moment he looked bleak. Then he shook his head as if dispelling a disturbing image. His voice softened. 'But you kept your head, and that's what matters. But don't *ever* do that again.'

'There was a time when I didn't know who to deal with first. I kept hearing the baby crying. Although I knew that meant it was probably okay, it still broke my heart not to be able to comfort it. And if I felt like that, God only knows how her mother felt. Any mother would have done the same for a child in distress.'

Logan's eyes darkened. 'Would they? Somehow I doubt it.'

Before Georgie could say anything else, Jamie and Lata joined them in the staffroom.

'I hear you did good,' Jamie said, switching on the kettle. 'All the casualties are doing well. Tell us about it.'

Georgie and Logan brought Jamie and Lata up to speed with what had happened. Georgie noticed Logan said nothing about her going down to the woman and child while they were in the car. No doubt he didn't want anyone to think he approved of her actions. Nevertheless, his praise of her was unstinting when he related the other, not so controversial part of the rescue.

'It must have been a bit nerve-racking,' Jamie said, holding out mugs of coffee to Georgie and Logan. 'With so many casualties.'

'It was a bit,' Georgie agreed. 'And I know I shouldn't say this, but it was exciting too. There's no doubt in my mind that if we hadn't been there with the helicopter, things might not have turned out so well.'

Lata touched Georgie gently on the arm. 'Weren't you scared at all? I know I would have been.'

'I don't think you would have, Lata. There's so much going on, it's impossible to think about yourself, even for a second.'

But now it was all over she couldn't stop shaking.

'I think I should take Georgie home,' Logan said, eyeing her with concern.

'I can drive myself home perfectly well,' Georgie insisted. 'I don't need everyone to treat me like some kid.'

Logan and Jamie exchanged glances. 'If you're sure,' Jamie eventually conceded. 'Don't come in until later tomorrow. And that's from Lizzie. You know how she can be if her nurses don't listen.'

Georgie did know. Lizzie would send her home in a heartbeat if she came in at the usual time tomorrow. The charge nurse, although easygoing most of the time, ruled the department with a rod of iron. She wouldn't want anyone on duty who wasn't fully rested.

'Suits me.' Georgie yawned. 'Right, then,' she said, getting to her feet. 'I'll see you all in the morning.'

Georgie tossed and turned as she thought about Logan. Throwing her bedclothes aside, she got up and went down to the kitchen. A cup of hot milk might be enough to send her back to sleep. She found her mother flicking through a magazine while she sipped her own hot drink.

'Couldn't sleep either, love?' Mary asked as Georgie tipped some milk into a pan. 'Can't say I blame you. It must have been quite an experience earlier.'

'Mmm. It was. But kind of exciting too. What's keeping you up?'

Mary folded her magazine and surveyed Georgie over the top of her reading glasses.

'I'm worried about you. Up until the last couple of weeks you seemed so much happier. As if you had been lit up from inside. I guess Logan was responsible for that?'

Georgie nodded slowly. It was no use pretending otherwise. Her mother knew her too well.

'But lately you seem unhappy again. And you haven't been out with Logan in a while. You've refused to talk to me about it. Has he hurt you? Because if he has, he'll have me to answer to.'

Georgie smiled. Her mother had always been over-protective, particularly so since Ian had died, but she hadn't really appreciated that Mary would have been anxious about her relationship—or lack of it—with Logan.

'He didn't dump me, if that's what you're thinking.' She poured the hot milk into a mug and sat down beside her mother at the kitchen table.

'Actually, Mum, he told me he's in love with me. He even asked me to marry him.'

Mary's eyes widened but she said nothing.

'I said no.'

'So he's not the man for you? I know it's early days yet and you haven't known each other very long, but perhaps you should give it more of a chance?'

Georgie felt tears thicken her throat. 'No, Mum. I do love him. With every fibre of my being. I didn't think I would ever love anyone again after Ian, but I do.'

'And you feel guilty? Oh, darling, I'm sure Ian would want you to be happy again. He loved you so much.'

Georgie shook her head. 'It's not that, Mum.'

'Then what is it? Go on, *mo ghràigh*, you can tell me.'

Georgie wrapped her fingers around her mug. 'I love him, but I couldn't spend the rest of my life with him.'

Mary raised an eyebrow in a silent question.

'The army is his life. When he finishes his stint here, he'll be going back. Back to the front line sometimes and every day he'll be putting his life in danger. I just can't spend every moment he's away wondering if I'll ever see him again. I can't put myself through that and I won't put Jess through it either. My life was fine before Logan came along. And it will be fine again. I have Jess and you and Kirk and that's better than nothing. Much better than nothing.' She forced a smile.

'Oh, Georgie, you can't run away from love.' Unconsciously, Mary echoed Sarah's words. 'Don't you know that by now? Even if you're not with him, do you think it will stop you worrying about him?'

'I'll get over him. As you said, we haven't known each other very long. In time what I feel for him will fade.'

'You don't really believe that, do you?' Mary said softly, reaching out and taking one of Georgie's hands in hers. 'What happened to my brave girl who used to know that nothing in this life is guaranteed and that happiness should be snatched whenever possible? If nothing else came out of Ian's death, surely it was that?'

'But what if I lose Logan too?' Georgie wailed, feeling the pent-up emotions of the last few weeks rise inside her. 'I couldn't bear it, Mum. It was hard enough to hold it all together after Ian. If it hadn't been for you and Jess, I don't think I would have been able to get through it. I never ever want to feel like that again. Can't you understand?'

Mary stood up and came to stand next to Georgie, placing an arm around her shoulder and hugging her close. 'Maybe you're not quite ready, love. Don't be too hard on yourself. If Logan is half the man I think he is, he'll be patient and will be there waiting for you when the time is right.'

Georgie allowed herself to rest against her mother. 'Maybe. I don't know. I just don't know if I'll ever feel differently. All I know is that I love him, and I wish I didn't.'

Back at his flat, Logan was restless. He couldn't settle to read and there was nothing on television that interested him. Images of Georgie kept whirling around his brain. Did she have any idea that she could have been killed?

He changed into his running gear and let himself out of his

flat. A ten-mile run would tire him out. Maybe he could exhaust himself so much he could keep Georgie out of his head.

But as he pounded the deserted streets he knew it was no use. Images of wavy red hair and grey-blue eyes the colour of a stormy sky kept coming into his mind. Georgie. He loved her. He'd never been more certain of anything in his life. But what could he offer her? Even if she had agreed to marry him, would he have been able to stick with it? What if he couldn't? None of his relationships had lasted more than a few months. Whenever they'd shown the remotest chance of getting serious, he had been out of there.

He followed the street along the river Clyde, concentrating on keeping his breathing regular. His mind drifted towards the woman who had abandoned him when he was two and the conversation he'd had with her. If he'd thought she would have been pleased to hear from him, he'd been very much mistaken. At least he had the information from her he needed. There was no family history that would prevent him having a family.

As a small boy, he'd let himself believe that his mother had given him up because she had been dying from some terrible disease and knew she had to find him a home before she died. Although, as he grew older, he'd known that it was just a romantic fantasy, somewhere in the back of his mind he had always wondered. But now he knew for sure that illness hadn't been the reason she had given him up. And that left him free to commit to Georgie. Except he didn't know if he could. Was that the real reason he didn't want to resign from the army? What if he was like his mother and couldn't deal with the responsibility of a family? What if something inside his soul was permanently damaged and he too would want to walk away—what then? How could he do that to Georgie and Jess? It wouldn't be fair. She had lost one husband and Jess a father. How would they cope with losing another, if not physically, then emotionally?

It was better to walk away. Georgie would get over him in time. But would he ever get over her? The answer almost tore him in two. He had never loved anyone the way he loved her, and he would never love anyone the same way again.

CHAPTER ELEVEN

'I NEED volunteers,' Lizzie announced during one of their shifts a few days later. 'To walk the West Highland Way in relays. It's for charity. Who's up for it?'

'In relays?' Georgie said puzzled. 'How will that work?'

'We divvy up the route into manageable sections. We each take one, preferably in twos or more, and walk it. Simple as that.'

'You mean we wait for each section to be completed and then start the next? Walking through the night? I've heard of people who have done it in the past. It sounds fun,' Sarah said. 'I'm up for it but I'd rather do the civilised daytime hours if possible. I'm happy to do up to thirty miles. I think Jamie and I could manage that in one day.'

'Great. I'll put the pair of you down for the middle section from Tarbet to the Devil's staircase, then. Anyone else?'

From the glint in Lizzie's eyes, it seemed as if no one was going to get out of it. *Volunteering* apparently didn't have the same meaning for Lizzie as it had for everyone else, Georgie thought with a grin.

'I'll do the Devil's Staircase to Kinlochleven,' Georgie offered. 'I know that part of the walk well. So if it has to be completed in fading light, I'm up for that. As long as my mum is happy to look after Jess, that is,' she added hastily.

'I'll do it with you,' Logan interjected quietly. Georgie was surprised. If anything, these last few days he had gone out of his way to avoid her when they weren't actually on a job together.

She ignored the speculative looks from her team. 'If you like,' she said casually.

The others were wheedled by Lizzie into volunteering until they had the full journey covered.

'If we all aim to finish our sections by five, six at the latest, then we can meet up at Loch Lomond for a barbeque to finish the day off. Everyone is welcome to bring their families. It's been a while since all of us were out together,' Lizzie added wistfully. 'And who knows when we'll get the chance again.'

'When do you go on maternity leave, Lizzie?' Sarah asked. 'It can't be that long now.'

'Another three months. I'm not planning to come back for another twelve after the baby's born. I want to make the most of those early days.'

'Who'll be covering for you while you're away?' Jamie asked. 'Has there been any decision made about that yet?'

Georgie caught the glance Lizzie sent her way. Lizzie still hadn't given up trying to persuade her to take on the post. It would be the right thing to do for Jess's sake. But would it be the right thing for her? She felt a wash of sadness as she thought about the future. It wouldn't be long before Logan was out of her life for good, and the thought made her heart ache.

Two weeks later and the day of the walk dawned. Lizzie, Sarah and Lata had spent any spare time between patients organising the barbeque they planned for the evening. As they couldn't rely on the weather, they had decided to hold it on a part of the lochside near a hotel. Several of the staff played musical instru-

ments and had agreed to bring them along. All in all, everyone
was looking forward to the day out.

The June day was better than everyone had hoped. As they
drove along the twisting road that ran along the loch and up into
the hills towards Loch Lomond, Georgie sneaked a glance at
Logan. Since they were doing the stretch together, it made
sense for them to share a car. This time Georgie had insisted
on taking hers and to her surprise Logan had agreed without a
murmur. Sarah and Jamie had taken Jess with them.

Something was bothering Logan—Georgie was sure of it.
Every now and again when he didn't think anyone was looking,
she would catch him frowning. Whereas before he had been an
extrovert, he had become distant, almost withdrawn, and she
wondered if the rest of the team had noticed. During the journey
they chatted easily about patients and the MERT service, but
Logan seemed guarded, and Georgie longed for the old easiness
of before. But could she blame him really? She had rejected
him, and for a man like Logan that must be hard to bear.

As usual, Glencoe was eerily magnificent. The glen still
seemed to be haunted with the ghosts of the past, but Georgie
loved the sense of history as well as the dramatic rise of the
mountains. It rarely failed to put life into perspective for her.

'Have you climbed all these mountains?' Logan asked.

'Many times. Some are more difficult than others, especially
in the winter.' She hesitated. 'I still get a thrill when I think of
being out there, competing against everything nature can throw
at me. I guess I never felt so alive as when I was climbing.'

'The way I feel when I'm doing my job,' Logan said quietly.

Georgie wasn't sure whether he was reprimanding her, or
trying to make her understand. And she did. No one had the
right to stop someone doing something they loved. Now that

she had lost her fear, she knew she would be back out on the mountains at every opportunity. Not being out there, hiding from what she loved most, had done something to her soul. Something she could never do to anyone else. Even if it meant putting her life at risk. And *she* had a young child to think of.

Suddenly it all became clear. Logan was who he was and she loved him not in despite of that but because of it. If that meant standing by while he risked his life doing something he loved, then that was the price she had to pay for loving him. Being without him in her life would slowly but surely eat away at her. She had lost her fear of climbing; she could also lose her fear of loving.

They pulled into the car park at the foot of the Devil's Staircase. The hike wasn't difficult and they would need no more than their walking boots and a small backpack each. Georgie smiled when she saw Logan pull out the emergency bag he always kept with him. They weren't so different after all.

As they made their way up the Devil's Staircase—a series of steps cut into the mountain—Georgie thought about what she should say to Logan. His expression as he climbed was closed, forbidding even.

She had to tell him she had changed her mind. She loved him and that was all that mattered. Living all over the world, worrying about him, would be dreadful, but not having him in her life would be worse still.

The path was busy with other walkers, some of whom tramped beside them for a chat along the way, others whom they passed with nothing more than a cheery hello. It wasn't really the time or place, Georgie thought, to talk to him. She would wait until the right opportunity presented itself.

Georgie revelled in being alone with Logan for the first time since the night of the stabbing. She pointed out the mountains to him and he told her about competing in the pentathlon. It was apparent that he had always loved being out of doors. Whenever she tried to get him to speak about his time in the army, he deftly turned the subject back to her.

Halfway through they arrived at the top. Beneath them the mountains stretched away to the right. To the left Loch Leven sparkled in the afternoon sunshine. The air was crystal sharp with only the faint scent of wildflowers on the breeze. Georgie felt truly happy for the first time in as long as she could remember.

'Let's stop here for lunch,' she suggested. 'It's all downhill after this.'

Logan nodded briefly and they found a flat piece of ground away from the main track. Georgie laid out the sandwiches and shortbread she had brought while Logan added flasks of coffee and juice, as well as some fruit.

They ate in companionable silence, enjoying the view. Georgie's heart was racing. She wanted to tell Logan she had changed her mind, but didn't know where to start.

'Logan…' she began hesitantly.

He turned to look at her, his expression unreadable.

'I made a mistake, I'm sorry.'

'A mistake? When?' He looked baffled, clearly thinking she was talking about a clinical error.

'Not at work.' This was more difficult than she had thought it would be. 'When I said I didn't want to be with you. I was wrong. I do want to be with you. Whatever that means. Wherever you go, I want go.'

To her surprise he turned away from her and looked out into the distance. This wasn't at all how she'd imagined it would be. Surely at this point he was supposed to be smiling and kissing her?

'No, you weren't wrong. You were right all along. It was me that made the mistake.'

Georgie could hardly believe her ears. Icy fingers clawed at her heart.

'I should never have asked you to love me,' Logan continued. 'I had no right.'

'But I do love you. And you were right. It was me who got it all wrong. I was scared. But I'm not now. At least, I am, I will always fear for you, but I'm more scared of being without you. I know that now.'

Slowly, he turned towards her and what she saw in his eyes made her heart freeze further.

'No. I'm sorry, Georgie. I've been thinking about it too. There is no future for us. I should never have spoken out.' He laughed ruefully. 'I guess I wasn't thinking straight.'

'And you are now?' Georgie could hardly get the words past her swollen throat.

He made as if he were going to touch her but dropped his hand. 'Trust me, Georgie, I'm not the man for you.'

Now she was really confused and didn't know what to say.

'I'm sorry, Georgie,' he said softly, and this time there was no mistaking the regret in his eyes. 'I wish I could feel differently, but I can't. At least…'

But Georgie wasn't listening any more. She had heard all she needed to. Wordlessly she began to pack up the remains of her picnic.

'I seem to have made a world-class fool of myself,' she said between frozen lips. 'Can we forget I ever said anything?'

Georgie knew she must've imagined it when she thought she saw pain flash in his eyes. She had made a mistake and the sooner Logan disappeared from her life, the better.

Back down at the barbeque site, preparations were well under way. Everyone had completed their share of the hike comfortably and spirits were high. Sarah had picked up Jess along with her son and brought her out to the loch. Jess and Calum were frequent playmates and were now absorbed by something down at the shore. Jamie and Sarah crouched next to them. Laughter drifted across the water.

The sight of her two colleagues still so much in love made her own sense of loss deeper. Just when she thought she had found love again it had all been snatched away and she couldn't understand why. The walk back down the hill had been tense. Both of them had made attempts at small talk but it had been clear that neither of them had had the heart for it and they'd eventually lapsed into silence.

The rest of the evening was hard, but Georgie managed to act as if she was enjoying herself, even if her heart felt as if it was breaking into little pieces. After they had eaten and Jess was listening to a story Sarah was telling Calum, Georgie strolled away from the main group and wandered off to the water's edge. The sun was sinking slowly in the sky, turning the loch red and gold. There was only the hint of a breeze, just enough for her to catch the scent of wood smoke in the air.

What had happened back there on the hill? Could Logan's feelings for her have changed so quickly? She simply could not accept that. He had told her he loved her and wanted to spend his life with her only two short weeks ago. If he hadn't meant it, what had he been up to? Did it have anything to do with the woman he had been seeing? The one who had phoned him when she had taken the call in the car? Was it possible Logan had been using her? No, she couldn't believe that. Not when every instinct in her body told her otherwise.

Logan watched the solitary figure of Georgie as she looked out over the loch. His heart ached for her. But he was doing the right thing, wasn't he? She'd get over him in time. It was better this way. She had made it clear she'd find it hard to accept his job in the army, to live with the fear every day, wondering whether he was still alive. And he couldn't blame her. She had suffered enough.

But, the relentless voice in his head was back. Was that the real reason? If he loved her, he could leave the army. But if she truly loved him, she would never have asked him to. The realisation hit him like a ton of bricks. That's what he was scared of. That she didn't love him enough. That one day she too would leave him. That was the true reason he had rejected her back on the hill. He was scared that she would leave him eventually, the way his mother had. He wasn't protecting Georgie. He was protecting himself.

Georgie heard the crunch of shells and whirled round to find Logan standing behind her.

'Logan,' she said flatly. 'I thought we had said everything we had to say.'

'I can't leave things between us like this. It's not fair. You deserve to know the truth. Even if there is no future for us, I can't pretend that I don't love you.'

The icy fingers around her heart began to melt. He did love her. Was that what he was saying? Now she was really confused. Logan was the last man she would ever have imagined not to be able to explain himself clearly.

He seemed to read her mind. 'I know I'm not making any sense. Look, can we go and sit somewhere—where no one can see us?'

She followed his gaze back up the shore. Sure enough, people were glancing their way. They were bound to be curious, although there wouldn't be an ounce of malice in their speculation. Nevertheless, whatever Logan had to tell her was best heard out of view.

They walked up the side of the loch a little until they found a rock to lean against. It had the dual advantage of shielding them from the wind as well as spectators. They sat down side by side, not touching. Georgie waited for Logan to continue.

'I haven't been honest with you,' he said. 'Remember when you asked me about my parents and I told you they died when I was young?'

She nodded.

'I lied to you.'

Georgie frowned. 'Lied to me? Why would you do that?'

'I don't know. I guess I was embarrassed, ashamed even.'

'Ashamed? I think you'd better tell me the whole story.' She turned and looked directly into his eyes.

'Talk to me, Logan,' she said softly. 'Remember that day in the plane? When you helped me face up to my physical fear? Can what you're about to tell me be any worse?'

A half-smile flickered across his lips. The beginnings of a beard roughened his jaw, emphasising his high cheekbones. Georgie would have given anything to pull him into her arms, but instinctively she knew this wasn't the time.

'My mother gave me up when I was two,' Logan continued after a pause. 'I spent the rest of my childhood either in foster-homes or a children's home. I don't know anything about my father. So, no, I don't have any family and I never did.'

Georgie was appalled. His mother had given him away? How could any woman do that to her two-year-old? It was beyond cruel.

She snuggled against him.

'I'm so sorry, Logan. I can't even begin to imagine what that was like.'

'And I can't imagine what it's like to have a family.' His tone lightened, but to Georgie's ears it felt forced. 'They say you don't miss what you never had.'

'Why did she give you up? Was she sick? What?'

'I didn't know why she did. No one ever told me. As a kid I used to imagine all sorts of scenarios as to why she couldn't keep me, no matter how much she'd wanted to, terminal illnesses included, but the truth is I was too much of a handful for her and she was very young.'

'All two-year-olds are a handful,' Georgie protested. 'Believe me, I know. But most mothers don't give their children away.'

He looked down at her. The naked pain in his eyes took her breath away. 'Then I must have been a particularly difficult two-year-old. I was always getting into things, getting into mischief. It was the same all the way through my childhood. None of my foster-parents kept me for longer than a year. Somehow they all seemed to find me too much to deal with. So I always assumed it was me.'

The image of a young Logan confused, baffled and hurt by constant rejection almost broke her heart.

'Why weren't you adopted?' she asked. 'Surely there were people who were desperate to take on a two-year-old.'

'That was part of the problem,' he said. 'It seems she refused to give me up for adoption at first. So I had to go to foster-homes. By the time she finally agreed, I was too old. From the age of six, I lived in children's homes. My behaviour deteriorated after that until there was no chance of anyone taking me on. I guess I didn't want anyone to try. There's only so much rejection a child can take.'

'Oh, Logan, I'm so very sorry,' Georgie said softly.

Logan looked at her, his eyes, darkening. 'I don't want or need your sympathy, Georgie,' he said warningly. 'After all, everything turned out for the best, didn't it? If I hadn't gone off the rails, my care worker would never have suggested the army cadets for me, and if I hadn't gone to the army cadets, I would never have realised what I wanted to do and made something of myself. So you see, Georgie, everything in life has a way of working out.'

'And your mother? Do you ever hear from her?'

'Funny you should say that,' Logan replied, and he couldn't quite keep the bitterness from his voice. 'I tried to contact her shortly after I met you.' He smiled down at her. 'Seeing the way you were with Jess brought back all the childhood fantasies of a loving mother who had to give me up, although she didn't want to. I left a message with the adoption agency asking that if she was still alive, could she get in touch.'

Georgie flinched from the look in his eyes. She had never seen him look so angry—and hurt—before. 'Needless to say, nothing. At least, not until a couple of weeks ago. She phoned me.'

Georgie waited quietly for him to continue. Something in his tone of voice told her the conversation hadn't been a happy one.

'She said that she was married and had a new family. Her husband knew nothing about me, and she wanted to keep it that way. She was sorry but there it was. She hoped I was happy and that I would have a good life. And that was it.'

He couldn't disguise the pain in his voice. What was it like to be rejected all over again? Even as an adult it must hurt. If she could have, Georgie would have taken his pain from him.

'Cow!' Georgie said forcibly.

Logan smiled wryly. 'I don't know, Georgie. It kind of helped in a funny way. I've spent most of my adult life thinking about her, wondering if she was okay. I imagined all sorts of scenarios and none of them turned out to be true. She was simply a woman who couldn't cope on her own with a young child. She thought she was doing the best for me by giving me up, and as it turned out she was right.'

'But not to want anything to do with you now…' Georgie was still angry for him.

'That's okay too. Because now I have you.'

Hope was blossoming somewhere deep inside Georgie. Now she understood why the army meant so much to him and why he didn't want to leave. It was the only family he had known. The only people he could trust never to let him down. Well, neither would she. She would be his family now. Whatever it took. If only he had explained all this weeks ago. But Logan wouldn't be who he was if he had. She knew his pride had held him back.

'If you want to stay in the army, that's okay, Logan,' she said. 'As long as I can be with you and Jess, I don't care. Families are where your loved ones are, regardless of where you are physically. I know that now.'

He stood up and pulled her into his arms. He squeezed her so tight he almost drove the breath from her body.

'When you turned me down, I was hurt. It made me think you couldn't love me as much as I loved you. And I couldn't accept that. I was also scared I would let you down. That I was incapable of love, that I was like my mother, unable to care enough to stick with a relationship whatever life brought. Then, just now, when I saw you down by the shore, looking so alone, I realised that I'd rather have whatever you could give me than nothing at all.'

She traced the contours of his face with her fingertips, hardly daring to breathe. 'What are you saying, Logan?'

He smiled down at her and the world became a brilliant place full of sunshine and promise.

'I can never stop loving you, not ever. I know now that what I was truly scared of was that you would stop loving me. I

thought about what you said. About losing Ian and how that had
torn you in two. I knew then it wasn't fair for you to take all
the risk of loving me if I couldn't take the risk of loving you.
But you wouldn't ever leave, would you? You're not the kind
of woman my mother is. Once you give your heart, you give it
for keeps. I'm right, aren't I?'

Georgie's answer was to lift her face to his, knowing he
would find the answer there.

Logan crushed her against him. 'We've been crazily stupid,
haven't we, Georgie?' he whispered into her hair. 'Both trying
to run from love, not knowing it was impossible.' He tipped her
chin with his finger until he could see into her eyes. 'When we
start our life together, I want it to be without secrets, without
fear that the past will come back to haunt us. I'm not running
any more, Georgie. Are you?'

EPILOGUE

GEORGIE stood nervously in the airport arrivals hall, clutching Jess's hand. The hall was packed with people waiting for their loved ones and her eyes welled up as she watched a woman fling her arms around the neck of a man as he scooped up the two small children who had gone running towards him with delighted cries of 'Daddy!'

She craned her neck, searching for the person she was waiting for. The last twelve months had been the longest of her life. Every day had been torture. Only sporadic phone calls and his letters had kept her sane. Logan had been home once during the last year, when they had married. But now, at last, he was coming home to her. This time for good. He had accepted the permanent job with MERT and while he had been finishing his time in the army she had been house-hunting for a home for the three of them. Or rather, she reminded herself as she dropped her hand to her stomach, the soon-to-be-four of them. In the end, she had taken on the department manager's job and, given her pregnancy, it had been the right decision. Lizzie would be returning from maternity leave, just as Georgie was going off on hers. It had all worked out rather well and there was still a place for her on the MERT team whenever she was ready to return to work.

The crowd parted and she saw him. Dressed for the last time in his military uniform, he looked unfamiliar and she caught her breath. Her heart started pounding as his eyes found hers. Time stood still as their gazes locked and then she was running towards him, pulling Jess with her.

Georgie flung herself into his arms and wrapped her legs around him. Stopping only to lift Jess into his arms too, he whirled her around and then there was laughter mixing with her tears.

'I've missed you. How I've missed you,' she cried as he rained kisses on her face. 'Don't you ever leave me again. You hear me.'

Jess was wriggling, wanting to be put down, and Logan lowered her gently to the floor.

He hugged Georgie tighter and she breathed in his familiar scent.

'I'm never going to leave you again, my love,' he whispered in her ear. 'Not as long as there is breath in my body.'

He released her, setting her down gently. The three of them stood in a circle, their arms wrapped around each other. 'My family,' he said, his voice catching. 'My child and my wife.' He touched her gently on the stomach. 'And how is this one doing?'

Georgie looked up at him, her heart full of love and gratitude. 'Your baby is doing just fine, Logan,' she whispered. 'C'mon, my dearest love, let's go home.'

MEDICAL™ 2-in-1

Coming next month

DARE SHE DATE THE DREAMY DOC?
by Sarah Morgan

Nurse Jenna Richards did *not* come all the way to Glenmore
to fall head-over-heels for the first sexy doctor she saw.
But what's a single mum to do when devastatingly
dreamy Dr Ryan McKinley has his eye on you?

DR DROP-DEAD GORGEOUS
by Emily Forbes

Plastic surgeon Ben McMahon has stepped out of Melbourne's
society pages and into nurse Maggie Petersen's life. He
sweeps Maggie well and truly off her feet— then the city's most
eligible bachelor discovers he's about to become a daddy!

HER BROODING ITALIAN SURGEON
by Fiona Lowe

Whilst Dr Abbie McFarlane appreciates eminent surgeon and
temporary colleague Leo Costa's skills, his famous Italian
charm she can do without! Abbie doesn't do flings – if she's
going to open her heart to Leo, she wants it to be for ever…

A FATHER FOR BABY ROSE
by Margaret Barker

Romance isn't something gorgeous, but guarded, surgeon
Yannis Karavolis cares about. Until he meets vulnerable
Cathy Meredith and her lovable infant daughter Rose,
Yannis begins to wonder whether fatherhood, marriage
and happiness could be his once more…

On sale 2nd July 2010

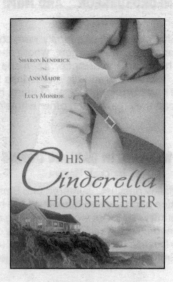
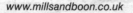

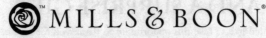

2 FREE BOOKS
AND A SURPRISE GIFT

We would like to take this opportunity to thank you for reading this Mills & Boon® book by offering you the chance to take TWO more specially selected books from the Medical™ series absolutely FREE! We're also making this offer to introduce you to the benefits of the Mills & Boon® Book Club™—

- **FREE home delivery**
- **FREE gifts and competitions**
- **FREE monthly Newsletter**
- **Exclusive Mills & Boon Book Club offers**
- **Books available before they're in the shops**

Accepting these FREE books and gift places you under no obligation to buy, you may cancel at any time, even after receiving your free books. Simply complete your details below and return the entire page to the address below. You don't even need a stamp!

YES Please send me 2 free Medical books and a surprise gift. I understand that unless you hear from me, I will receive 5 superb new stories every month including two 2-in-1 books priced at £4.99 each and a single book priced at £3.19, postage and packing free. I am under no obligation to purchase any books and may cancel my subscription at any time. The free books and gift will be mine to keep in any case.

Ms/Mrs/Miss/Mr _____ Initials _____

Surname _____

Address _____

_____ Postcode _____

E-mail _____

Send this whole page to: Mills & Boon Book Club, Free Book Offer, FREEPOST NAT 10298, Richmond, TW9 1BR